DreamWorks

Trolls

#2

"Put Your Hair in the Air!"

PAPERCUTZ

NEW YORK

MORE GREAT GRAPHIC NOVEL SERIES AVAILABLE FROM PAPERCUTZ

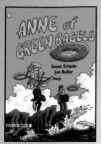

ANNE of GREEN BAGELS
Susan Schade
Jon Buller
PAPERCUTZ
ANNE OF GREEN BAGELS #1

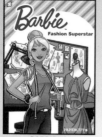

Barbie
Fashion Superstar
PAPERCUTZ
BARBIE #1

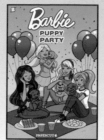

Barbie
PUPPY PARTY
PAPERCUTZ
BARBIE PUPPY PARTY

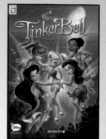

TinkerBell
PAPERCUTZ
DISNEY FAIRIES #18

JOHN STEVEN GURNEY
Fuzzy Baseball
FUZZY BASEBALL

GARFIELD
APPRENTICE SORCERER
PAPERCUTZ
THE GARFIELD SHOW #6

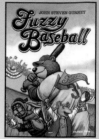

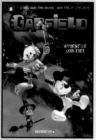

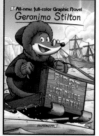

All-new, full-color Graphic Novel
Geronimo Stilton
FIRST TO THE LAST PLACE ON EARTH!
PAPERCUTZ
GERONIMO STILTON #18

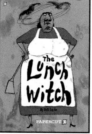

The Lunch Witch
By Deb Lucke
PAPERCUTZ
THE LUNCH WITCH #1

MINNIE & DAISY
BEST FRIENDS FOREVER
PAPERCUTZ
MINNIE & DAISY #1

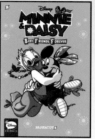

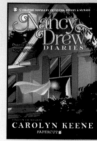

Nancy Drew
DIARIES
CAROLYN KEENE
PAPERCUTZ
NANCY DREW DIARIES #7

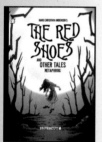

HANS CHRISTIAN ANDERSEN'S
THE RED SHOES
AND OTHER TALES
METAPHROG
PAPERCUTZ
THE RED SHOES

Susan Schade
Jon Buller
Scarlett
Star on the Run
PAPERCUTZ
SCARLETT

William
The Sisters
PAPERCUTZ
THE SISTERS #1

THE WILD SMURF
THE SMURFS #21

All-new, full-color Graphic Novel
Thea Stilton
THE THEA SISTERS
MYSTERY AT SEA
PAPERCUTZ
THEA STILTON #6

THE SMURFS, MINNIE & DAISY, DISNEY FAIRIES, THE GARFIELD SHOW, BARBIE and TROLLS graphic novels are available for $7.99 in paperback, and $12.99 in hardcover. GERONIMO STILTON and THEA STILTON graphic novels are available for $9.99 in hardcover only. FUZZY BASEBALL and NANCY DREW DIARIES graphic novels are available for $9.99 in paperback only. THE LUNCH WITCH, SCARLETT, and ANNE OF GREEN BAGELS graphic novels are available for $14.99 in paperback only. THE RED SHOES graphic novel is available for $12.99 in hardcover only. Available from booksellers everywhere. You can also order online from www.papercutz.com. Or call 1-800-886-1223, Monday through Friday, 9–5 EST. MC, Visa, and AmEx accepted. To order by mail, please add $4.00 for postage and handling for first book ordered, $1.00 for each additional book and make check payable to NBM Publishing. Send to: Papercutz, 160 Broadway, Suite 700, East Wing, New York, NY 10038.

THE SMURFS, THE GARFIELD SHOW, BARBIE, TROLLS, GERONIMO STILTON, THEA STILTON, FUZZY BASEBALL, THE LUNCH WITCH, NANCY DREW DIARIES, THE RED SHOES, ANNE OF GREEN BAGELS, and SCARLETT graphic novels are also available wherever e-books are sold.

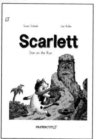

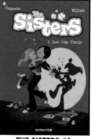

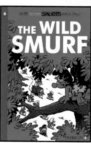

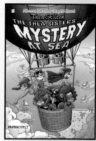

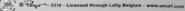

DreamWorks

Trolls

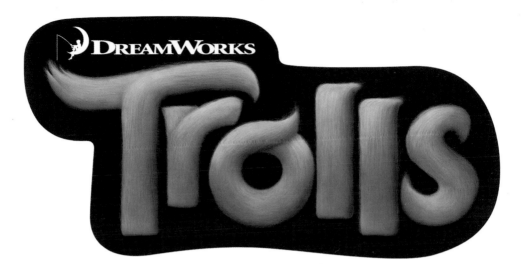

TABLE OF CONTENTS

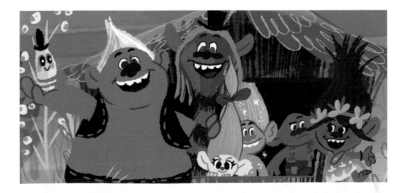

#2

"Put Your Hair in the Air!"

"Lost The Beat"
Script: Dave Scheidt
Art and Colors: Kathryn Hudson
Letters: Tom Orzechowski

"Roommates"
Script: Barry Hutchinson
Art: Miguel Fernandez
Colors: GFB

"Top of the Morning (and Night) to You!"
Script: Dave Scheidt
Art and Colors: Kathryn Hudson
Letters: Tom Orzechowski

"Wakey-Wakey"
Script: Dave Scheidt
Art and Colors: Kathryn Hudson
Letters: Tom Orzechowski

"Bad Hair Day"
Script: Barry Hutchinson
Pencils: Angel Rodriguez
Inks: Ferran Rodriguez
Colors: GFB

"Surfin' Contest"
Script: Dave Scheidt
Art and Colors: Kathryn Hudson
Letters: Tom Orzechowski

"The Dinkles Drop"
Script: Barry Hutchinson
Art and Colors: Artful Doodlers

"Class Visitors"
Script: Dave Scheidt
Art and Colors: Kathryn Hudson
Letters: Tom Orzechowski

THE SISTERS #2 "Doing it Our Way!" Preview
Story: Christophe Cazenove & William
Art: William

Production — Dawn K. Guzzo
Production Coordinator — Sasha Kimiatek
Editor — Robert V. Conte
Assistant Managing Editor — Jeff Whitman
Special Thanks to DreamWorks Animation —
Corinne Combs, Lawrence "Shifty" Hamashima,
Barbara Layman, Mike Sund, Alex Ward,
John Tanzer, and Megan Startz
Jim Salicrup
Editor-in-Chief

ISBN: 978-1-62991-718-4 Paperback Edition
ISBN: 978-1-62991-719-1 Hardcover Edition

Printed in Korea
April 2017

Papercutz books may be purchased for business or promotional use.
For information on bulk purchases please contact Macmillan Corporate
and Premium Sales Department at (800) 221-7945 x5442.

Distributed by Macmillan
First Printing

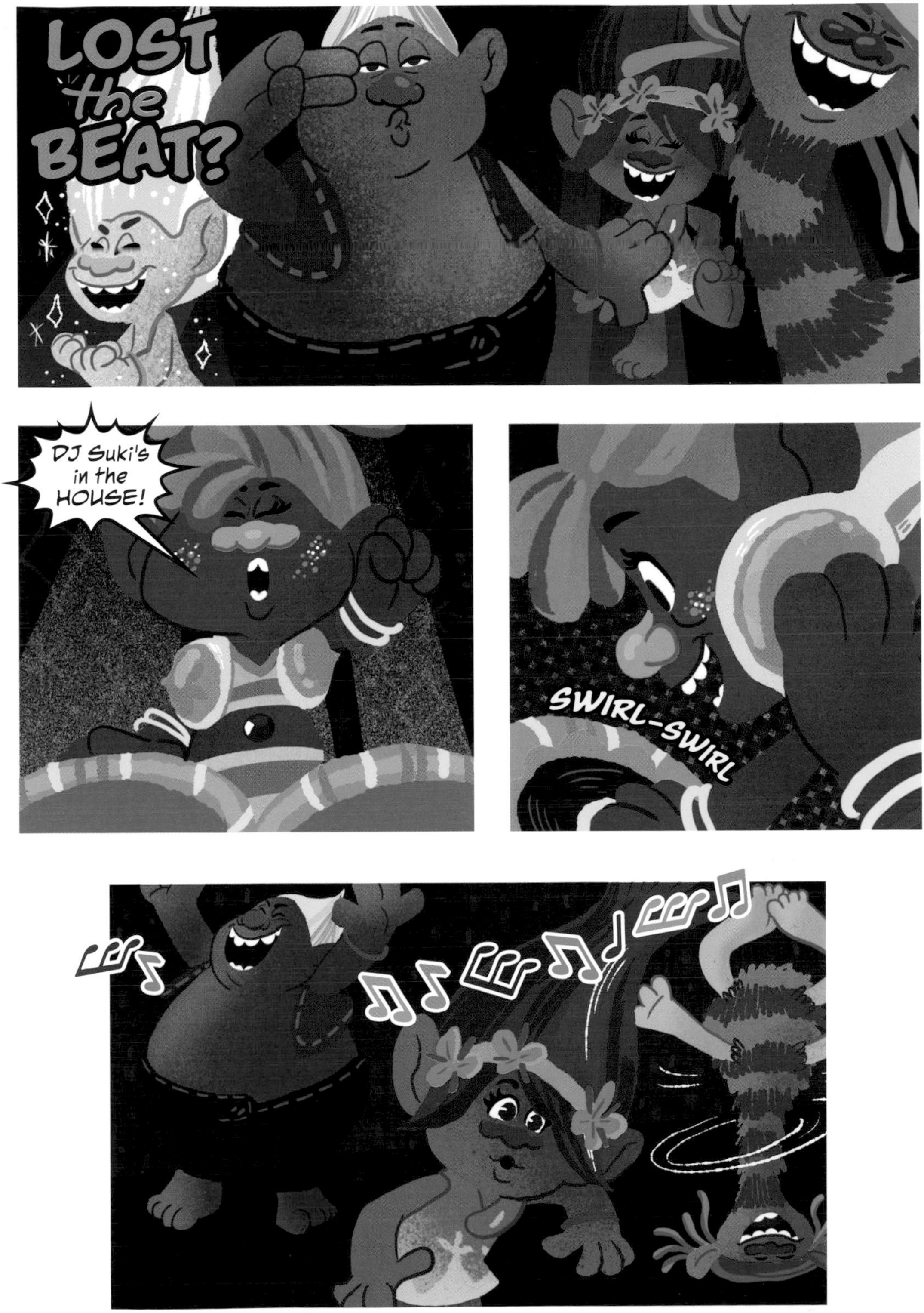
LOST the BEAT?
DJ Suki's in the HOUSE!
SWIRL-SWIRL

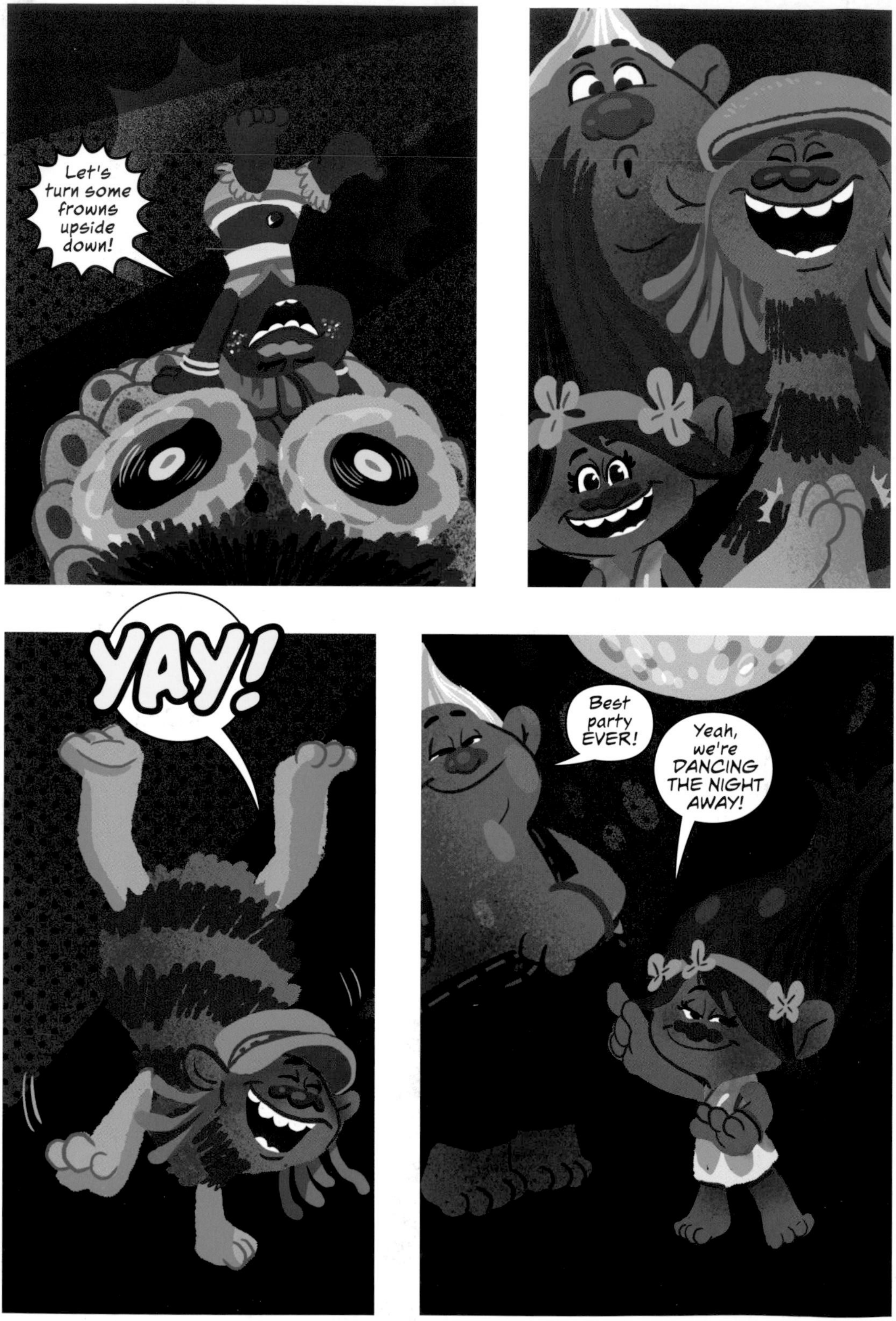
Let's turn some frowns upside down!
YAY!
Best party EVER!
Yeah, we're DANCING THE NIGHT AWAY!

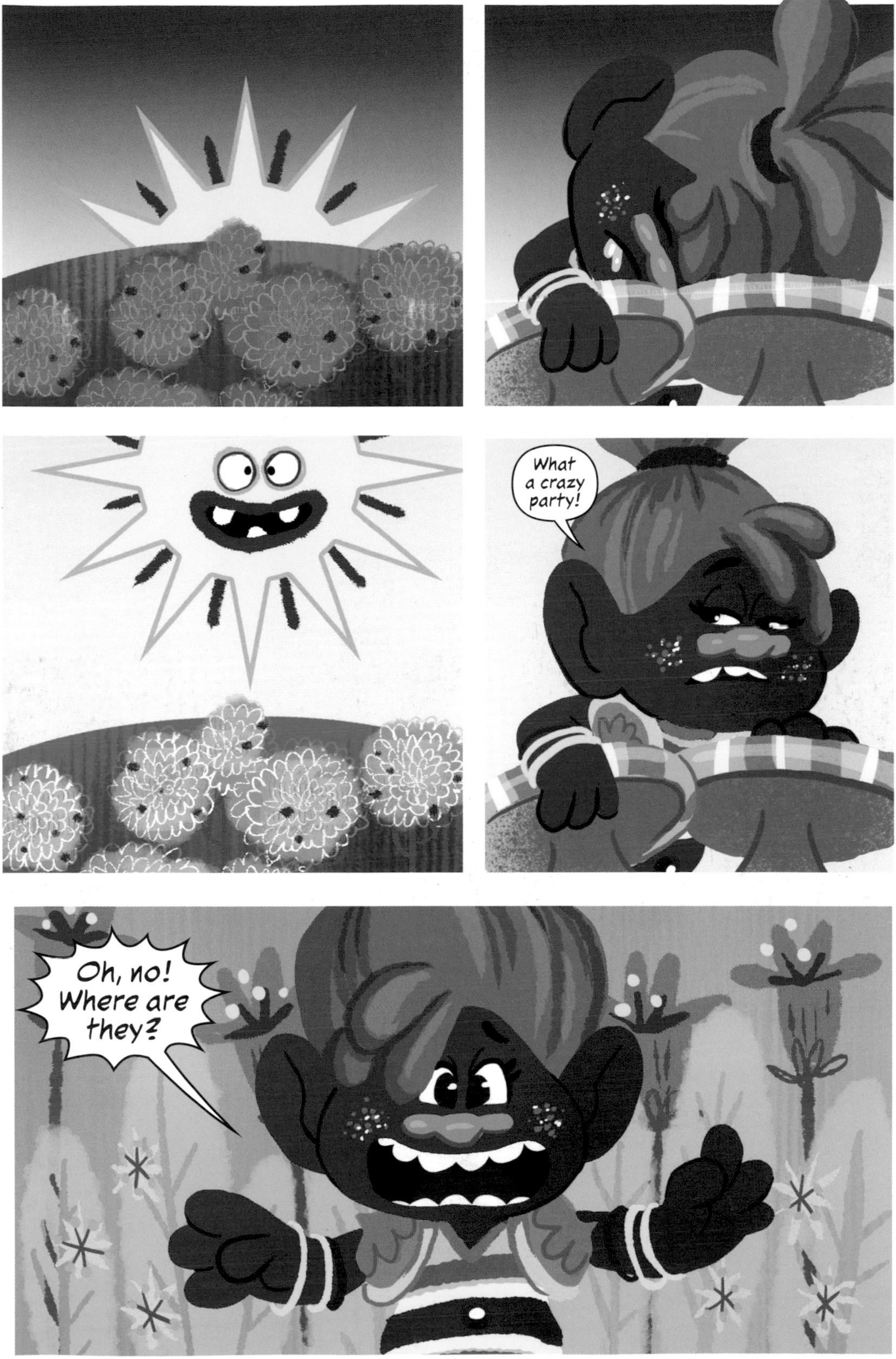
What a crazy party!
Oh, no! Where are they?

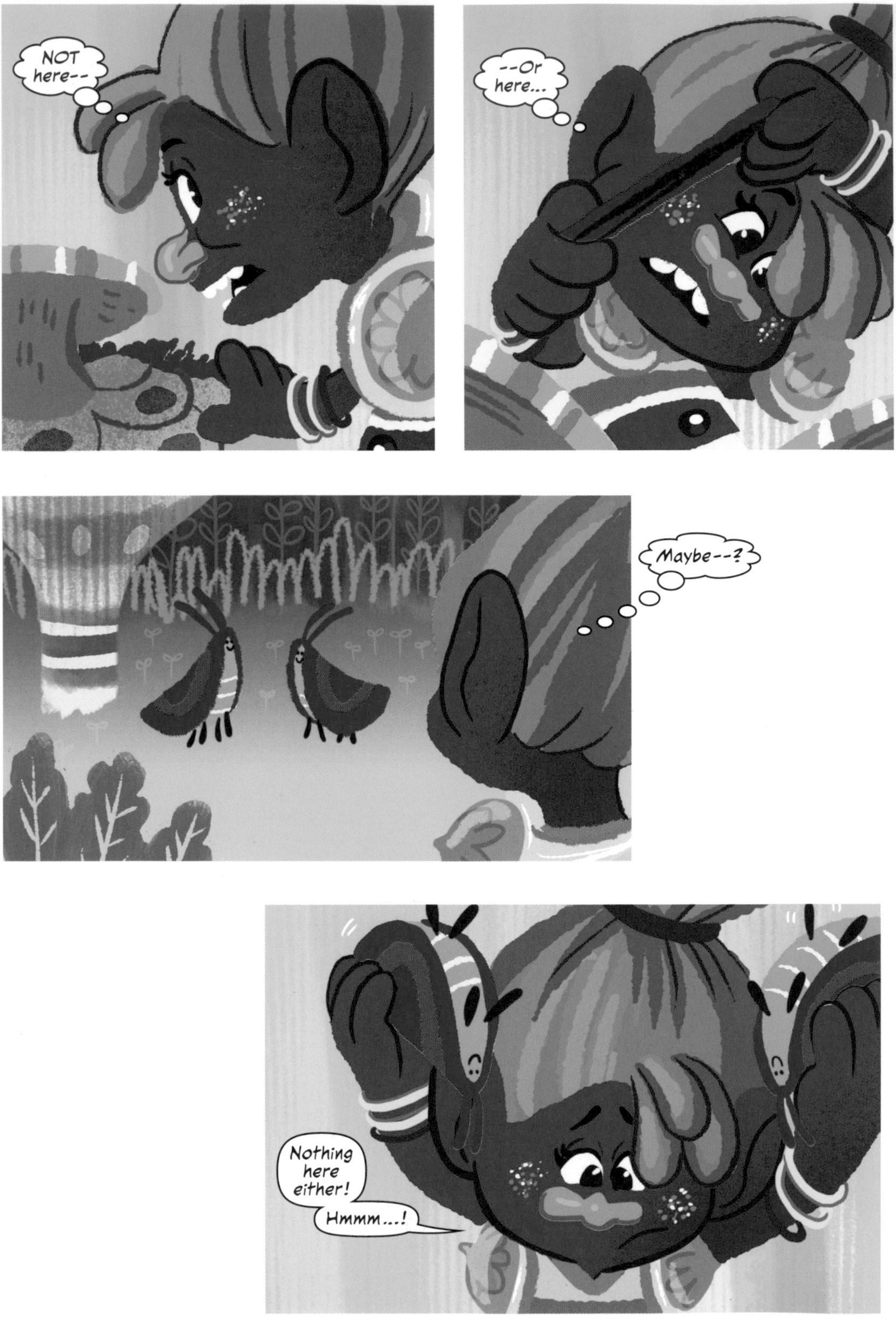
NOT here--
--Or here...
Maybe--?
Nothing here either!
Hmmm...!

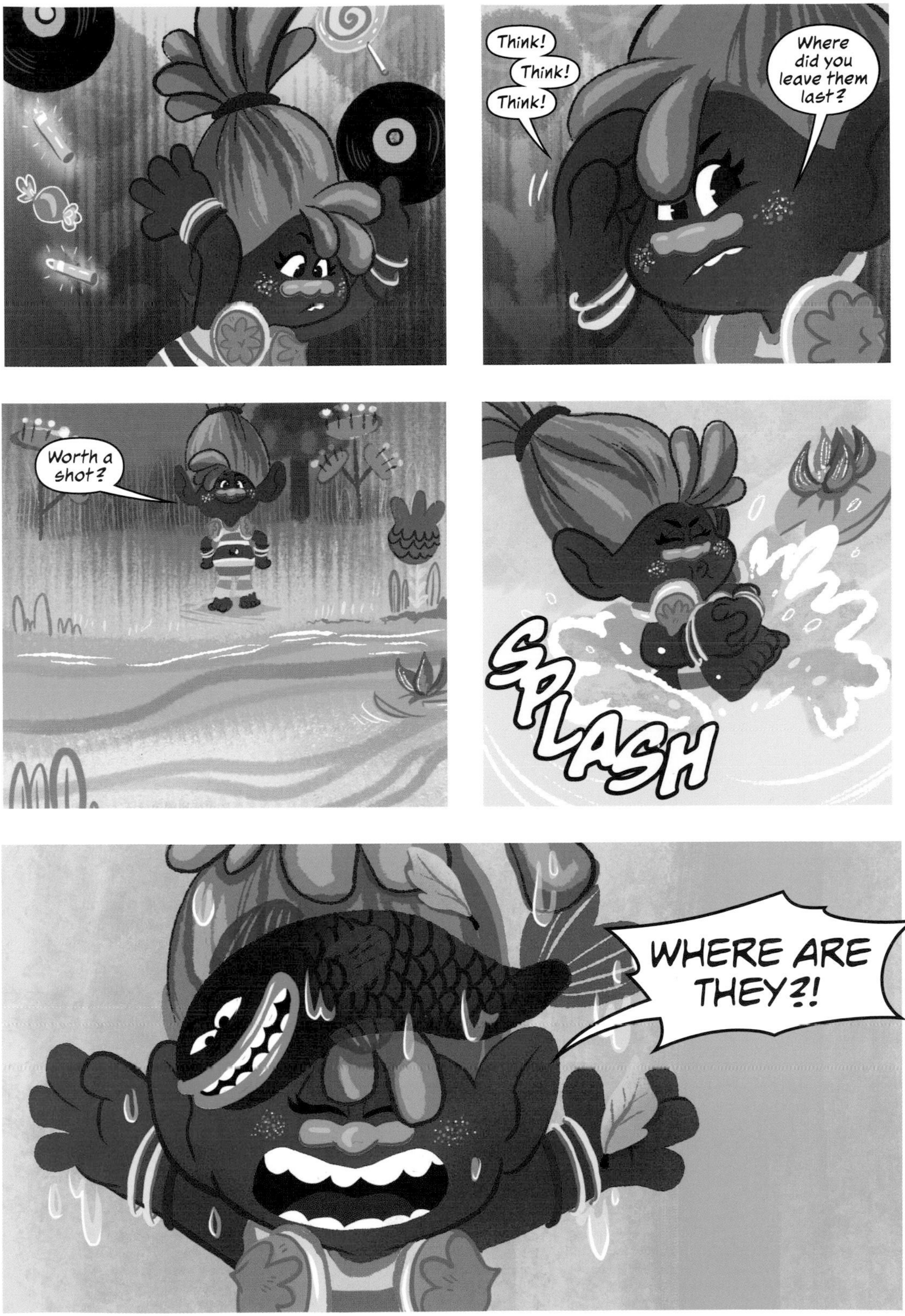
Think!
Think!
Think!
Where did you leave them last?
Worth a shot?
SPLASH
WHERE ARE THEY?!

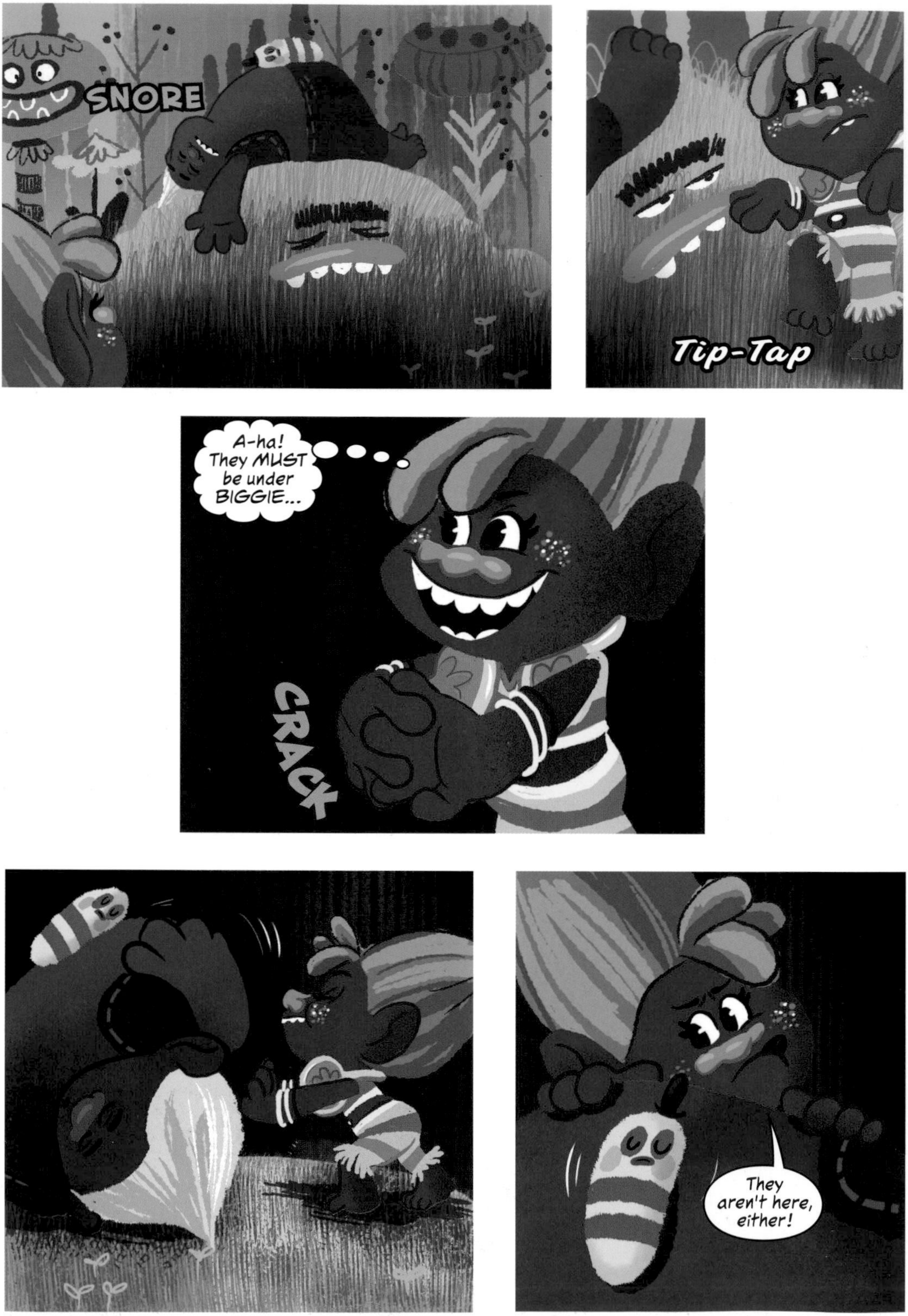
SNORE
Tip-Tap
A-ha! They MUST be under BIGGIE...
CRACK
They aren't here, either!

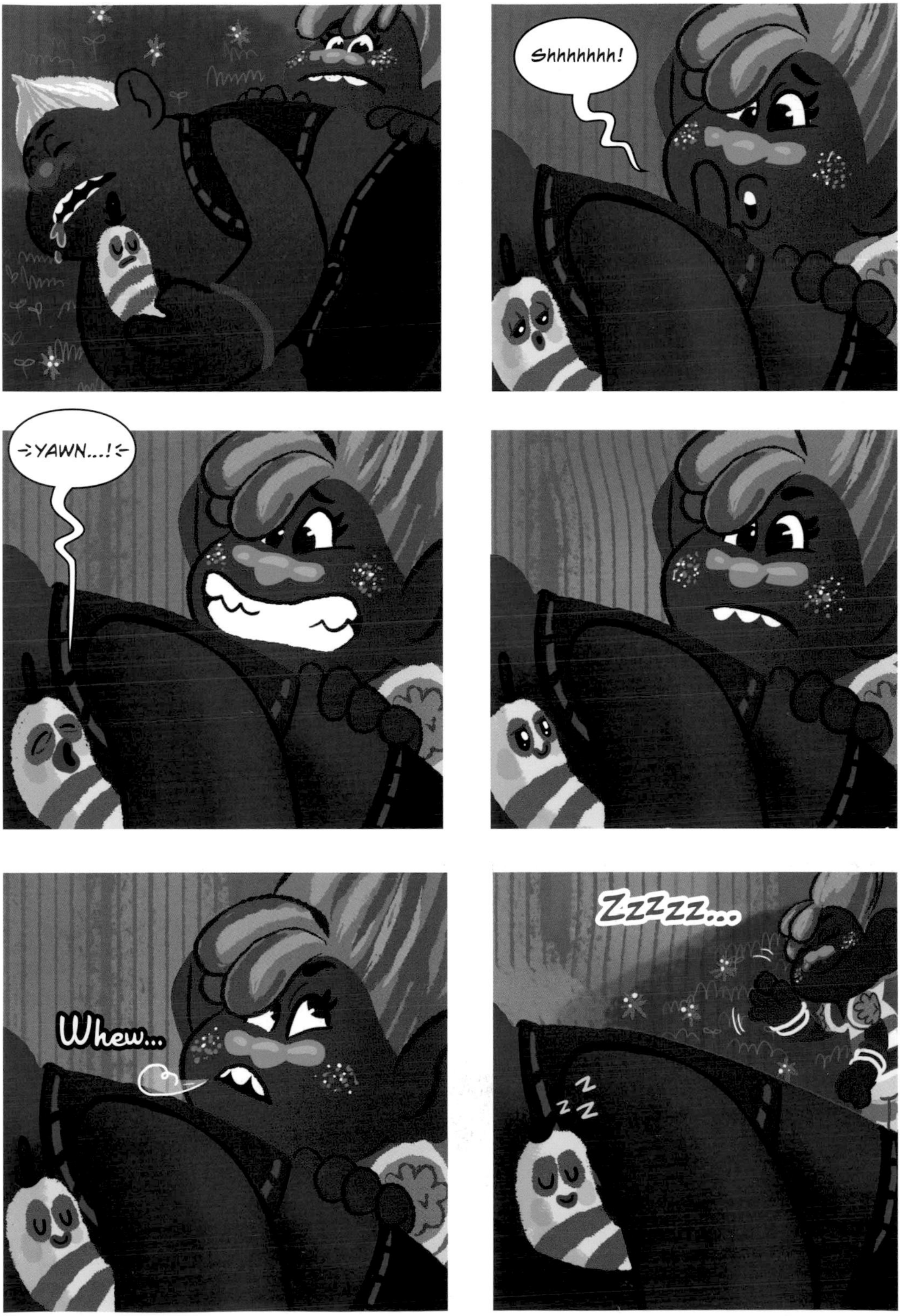
Shhhhhhh!
YAWN...!
Whew...
Zzzzz...
Z
Z Z

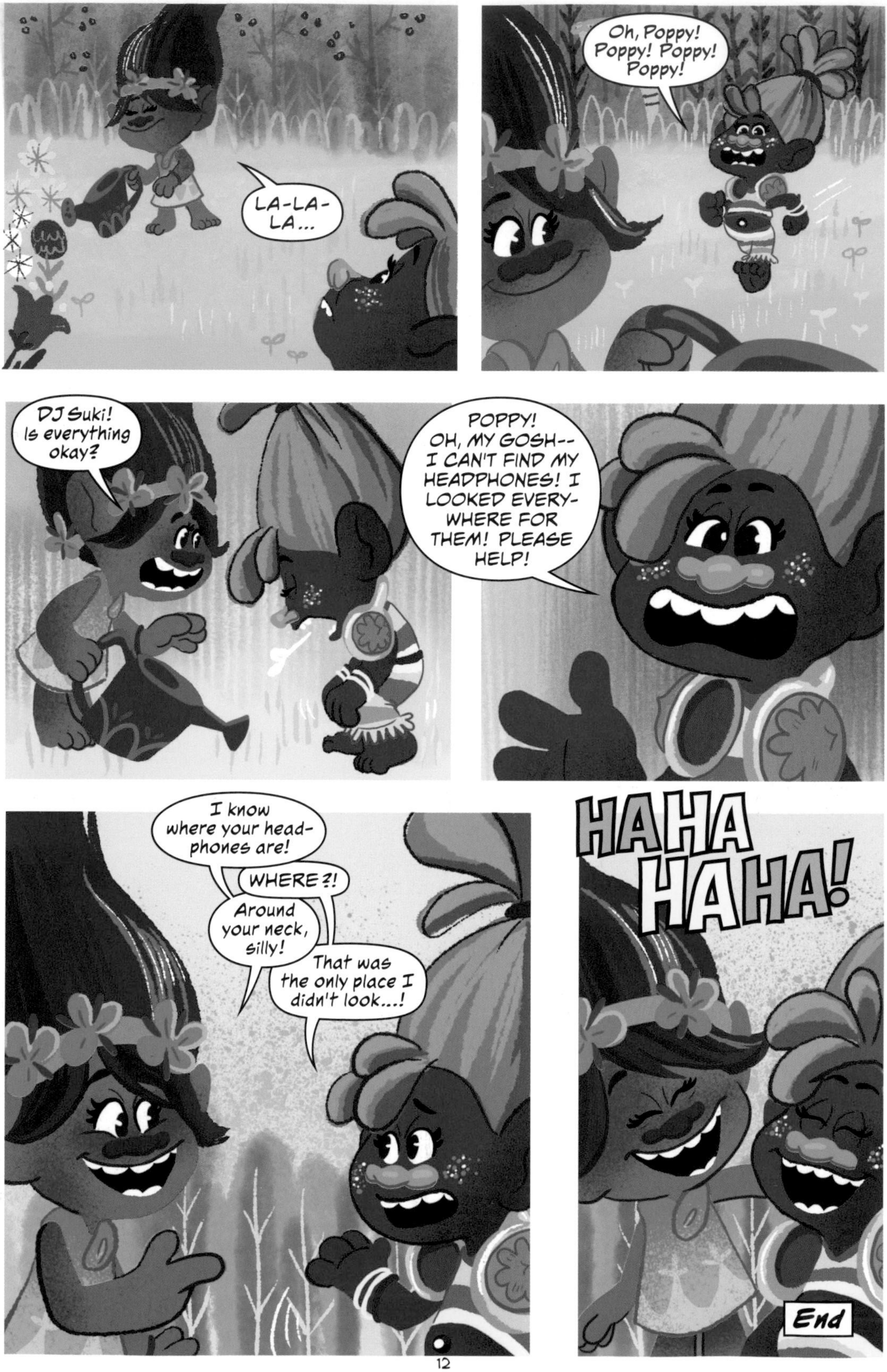
LA-LA-LA...
Oh, Poppy! Poppy! Poppy! Poppy!
DJ Suki! Is everything okay?
POPPY! OH, MY GOSH-- I CAN'T FIND MY HEADPHONES! I LOOKED EVERY-WHERE FOR THEM! PLEASE HELP!
I know where your head-phones are!
WHERE?!
Around your neck, silly!
That was the only place I didn't look...!
HAHA HAHA!
End

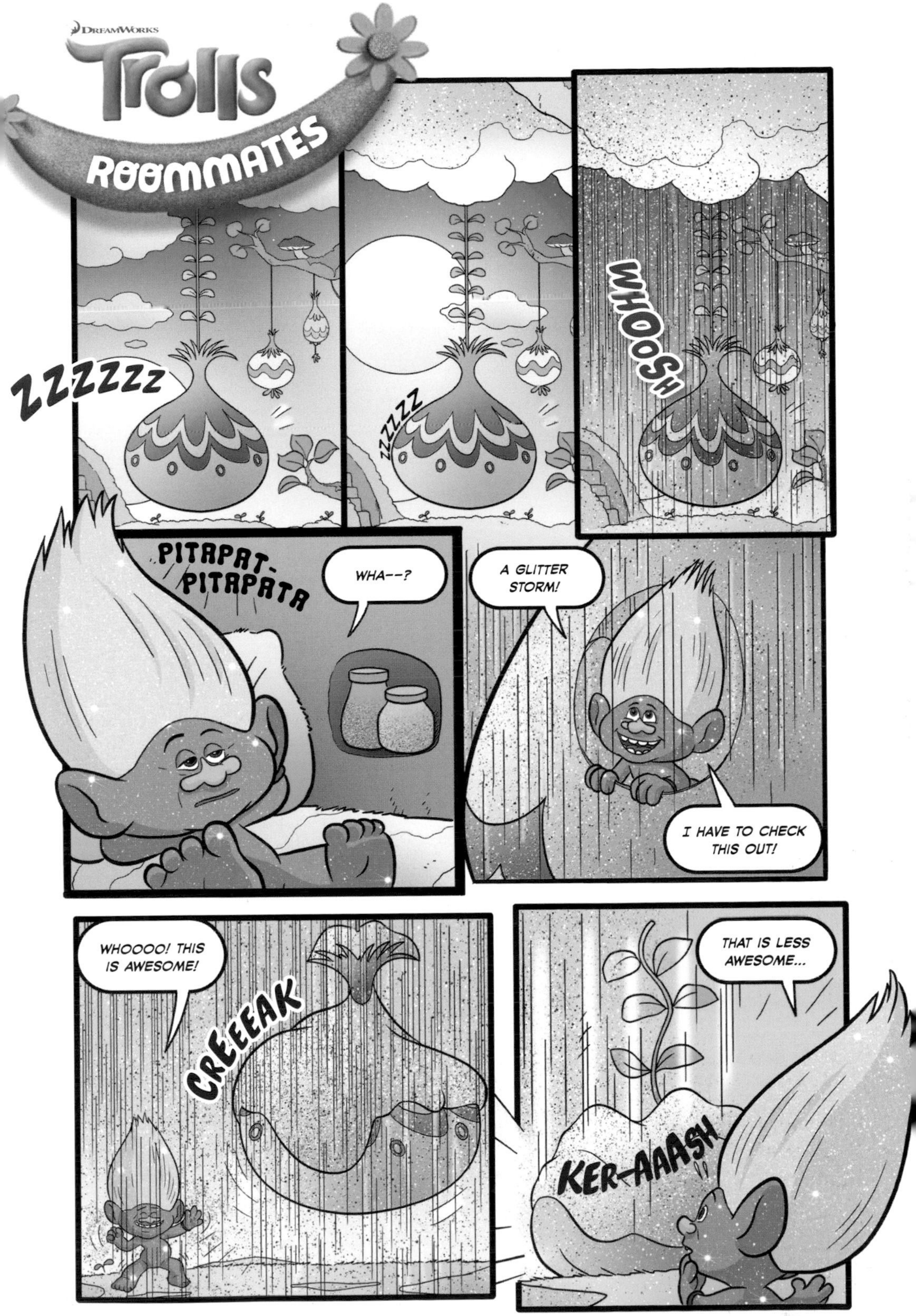
DreamWorks
Trolls
ROOMMATES
ZZZZZZ
ZZZZZ
WHOOSH
PITAPAT-
PITAPATA
WHA--?
A GLITTER STORM!
I HAVE TO CHECK THIS OUT!
WHOOOO! THIS IS AWESOME!
CREEEAK
THAT IS LESS AWESOME...
KER-AAASH

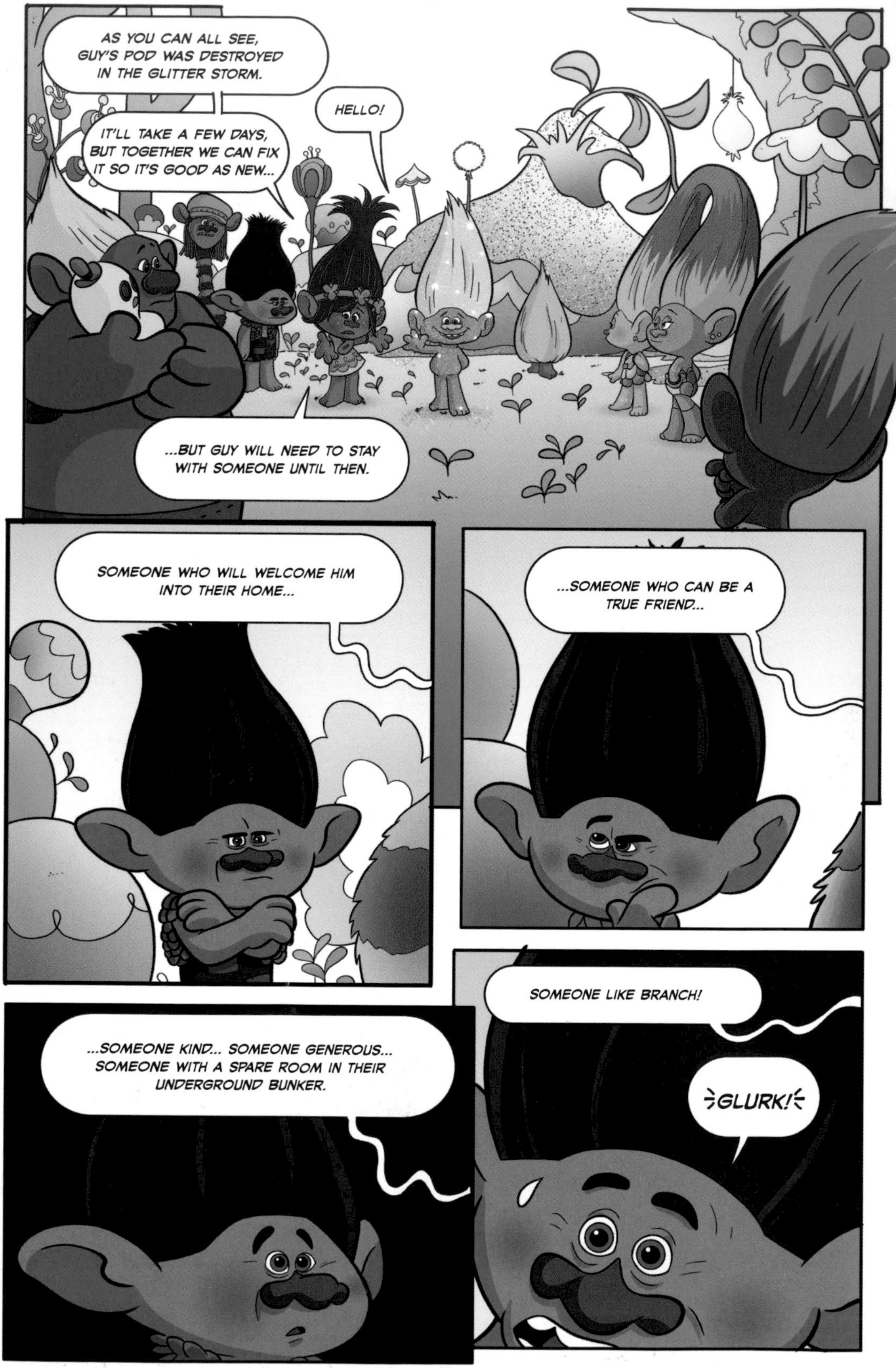
AS YOU CAN ALL SEE, GUY'S POD WAS DESTROYED IN THE GLITTER STORM.
IT'LL TAKE A FEW DAYS, BUT TOGETHER WE CAN FIX IT SO IT'S GOOD AS NEW...
HELLO!
...BUT GUY WILL NEED TO STAY WITH SOMEONE UNTIL THEN.
SOMEONE WHO WILL WELCOME HIM INTO THEIR HOME...
...SOMEONE WHO CAN BE A TRUE FRIEND...
...SOMEONE KIND... SOMEONE GENEROUS... SOMEONE WITH A SPARE ROOM IN THEIR UNDERGROUND BUNKER.
SOMEONE LIKE BRANCH!
GLURK!

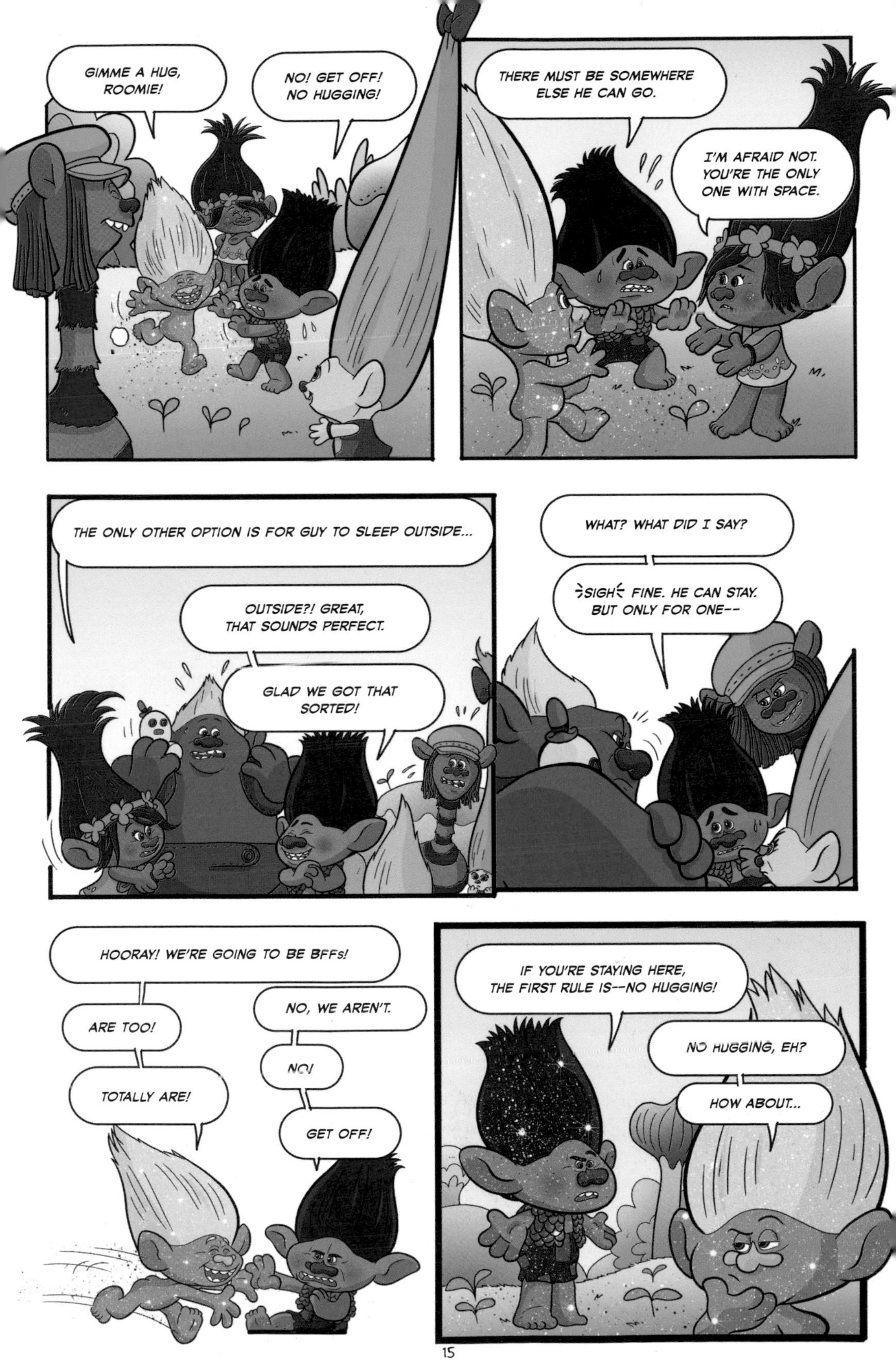
GIMME A HUG, ROOMIE!
NO! GET OFF! NO HUGGING!
THERE MUST BE SOMEWHERE ELSE HE CAN GO.
I'M AFRAID NOT. YOU'RE THE ONLY ONE WITH SPACE.
THE ONLY OTHER OPTION IS FOR GUY TO SLEEP OUTSIDE...
OUTSIDE?! GREAT, THAT SOUNDS PERFECT.
GLAD WE GOT THAT SORTED!
WHAT? WHAT DID I SAY?
SIGH FINE. HE CAN STAY. BUT ONLY FOR ONE--
HOORAY! WE'RE GOING TO BE BFFs!
ARE TOO!
TOTALLY ARE!
NO, WE AREN'T.
NO!
GET OFF!
IF YOU'RE STAYING HERE, THE FIRST RULE IS--NO HUGGING!
NO HUGGING, EH?
HOW ABOUT...

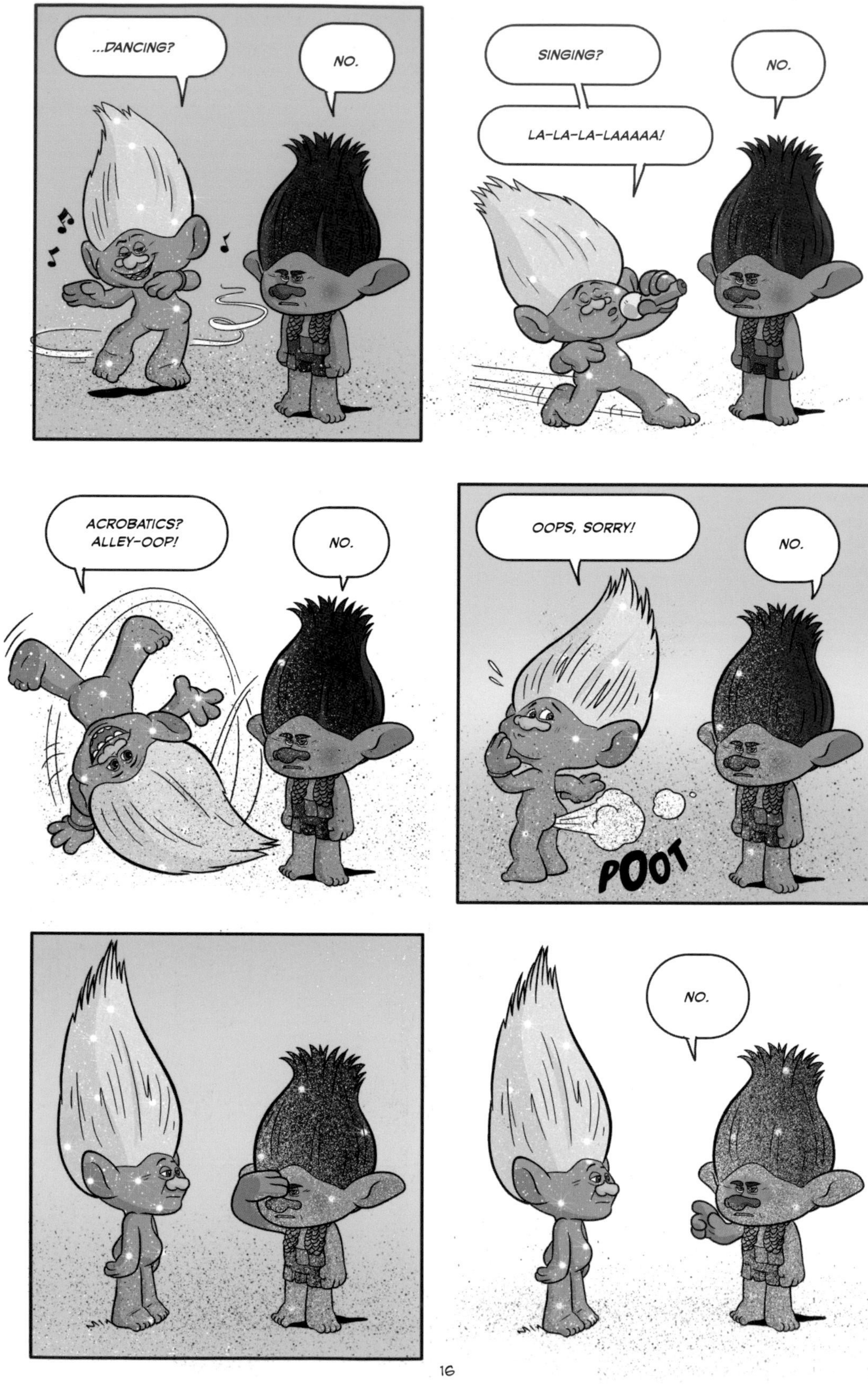
...DANCING?
NO.
SINGING?
LA-LA-LA-LAAAAA!
NO.
ACROBATICS? ALLEY-OOP!
NO.
OOPS, SORRY!
POOT
NO.
NO.

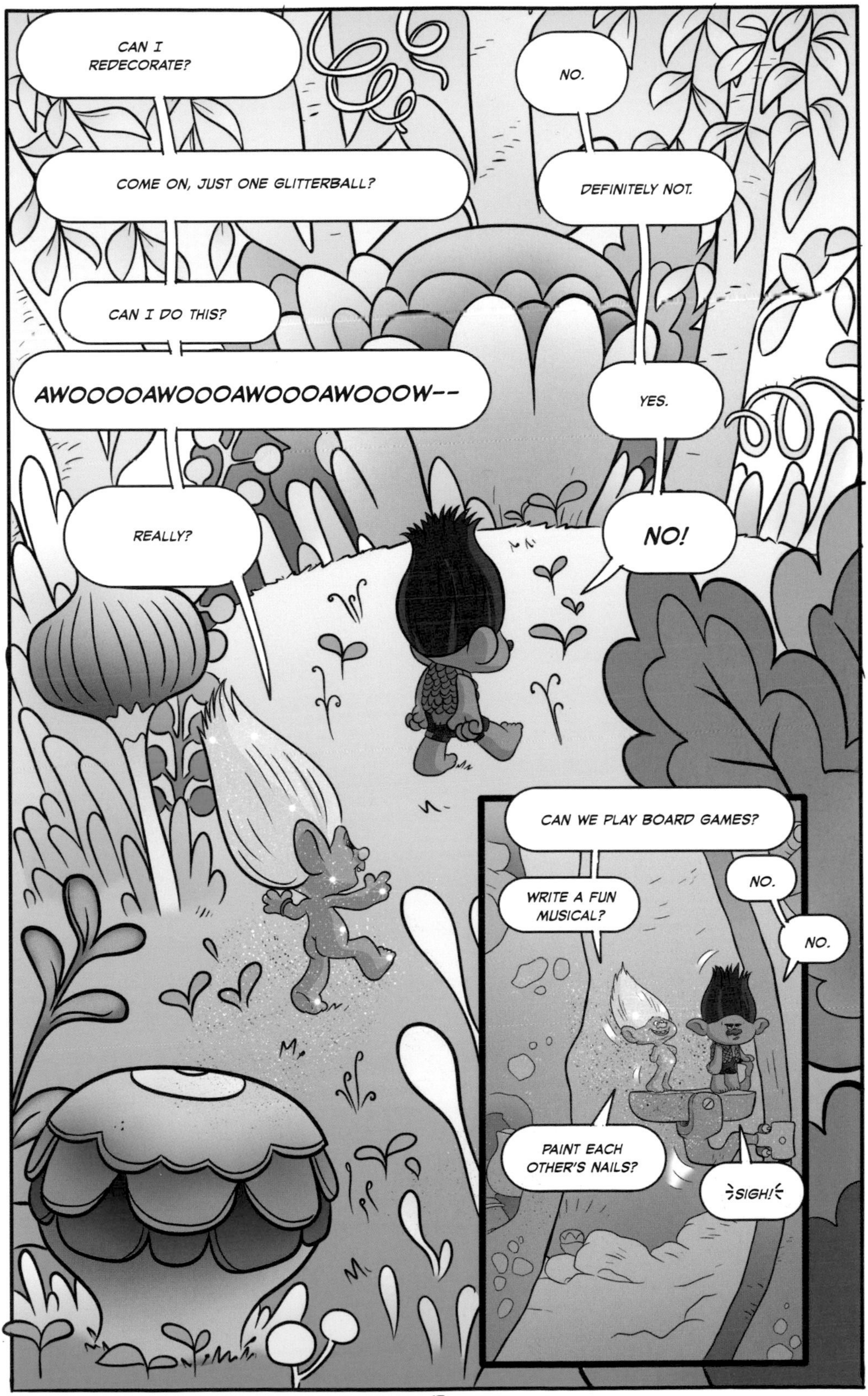
CAN I REDECORATE?
NO.
COME ON, JUST ONE GLITTERBALL?
DEFINITELY NOT.
CAN I DO THIS?
AWOOOOAWOOOAWOOOAWOOOW--
YES.
REALLY?
NO!
CAN WE PLAY BOARD GAMES?
NO.
WRITE A FUN MUSICAL?
NO.
PAINT EACH OTHER'S NAILS?
SIGH!

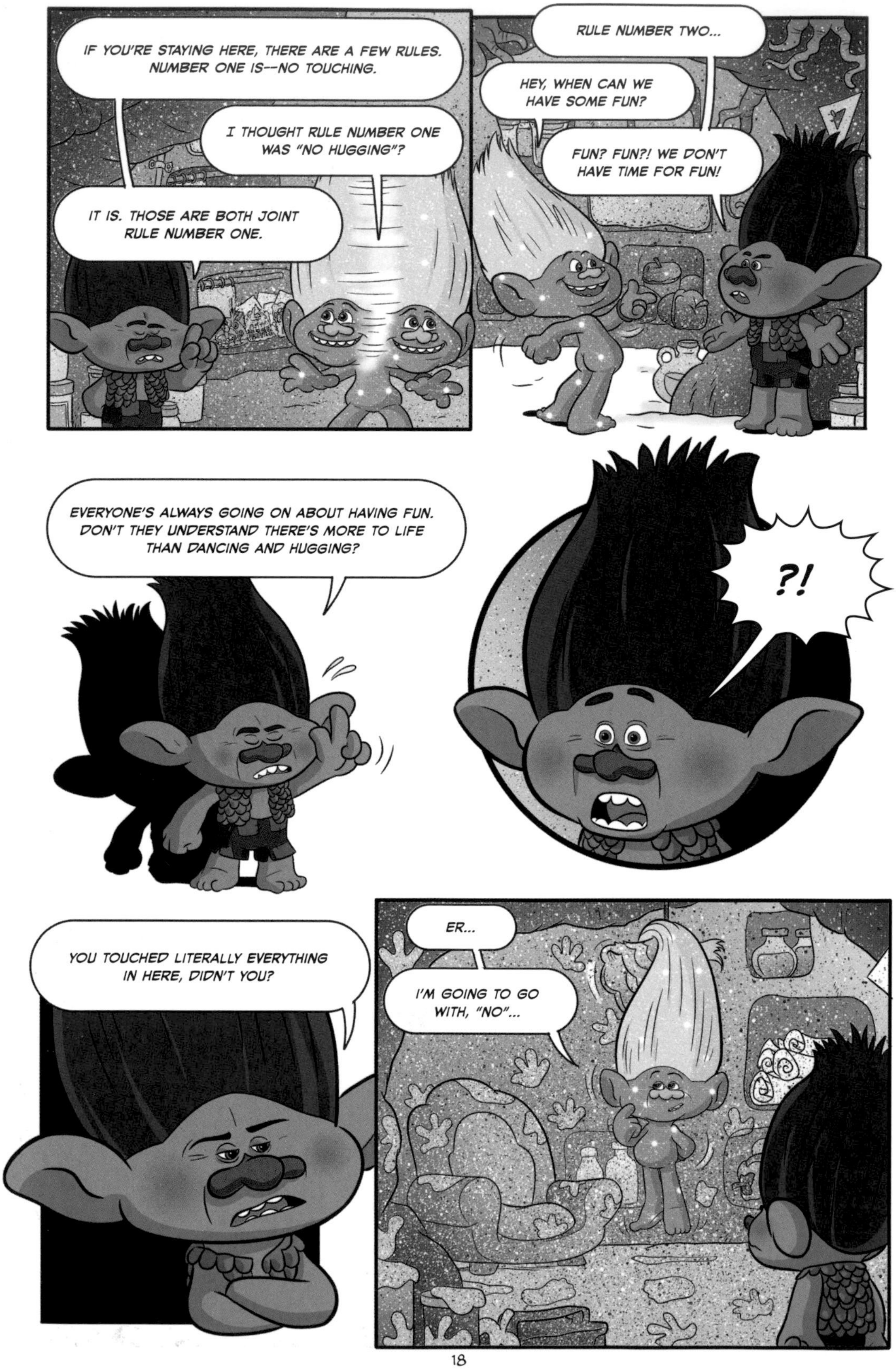
IF YOU'RE STAYING HERE, THERE ARE A FEW RULES. NUMBER ONE IS--NO TOUCHING.
I THOUGHT RULE NUMBER ONE WAS "NO HUGGING"?
IT IS. THOSE ARE BOTH JOINT RULE NUMBER ONE.
RULE NUMBER TWO...
HEY, WHEN CAN WE HAVE SOME FUN?
FUN? FUN?! WE DON'T HAVE TIME FOR FUN!
EVERYONE'S ALWAYS GOING ON ABOUT HAVING FUN. DON'T THEY UNDERSTAND THERE'S MORE TO LIFE THAN DANCING AND HUGGING?
?!
YOU TOUCHED LITERALLY EVERYTHING IN HERE, DIDN'T YOU?
ER...
I'M GOING TO GO WITH, "NO"...

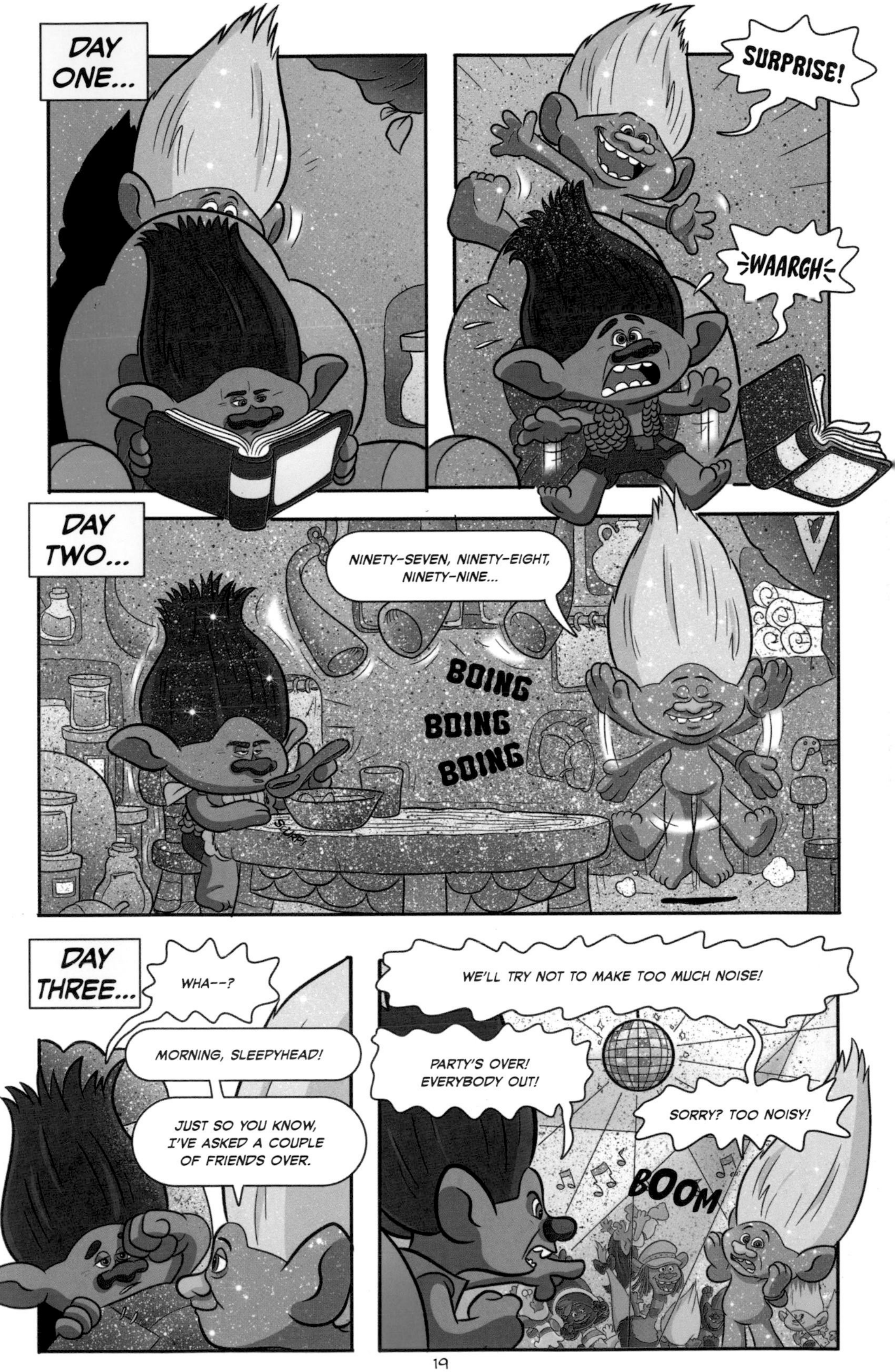
DAY ONE...
SURPRISE!
WAARGH
DAY TWO...
NINETY-SEVEN, NINETY-EIGHT, NINETY-NINE...
BOING
BOING
BOING
DAY THREE...
WHA--?
MORNING, SLEEPYHEAD!
JUST SO YOU KNOW, I'VE ASKED A COUPLE OF FRIENDS OVER.
WE'LL TRY NOT TO MAKE TOO MUCH NOISE!
PARTY'S OVER! EVERYBODY OUT!
SORRY? TOO NOISY!
BOOM

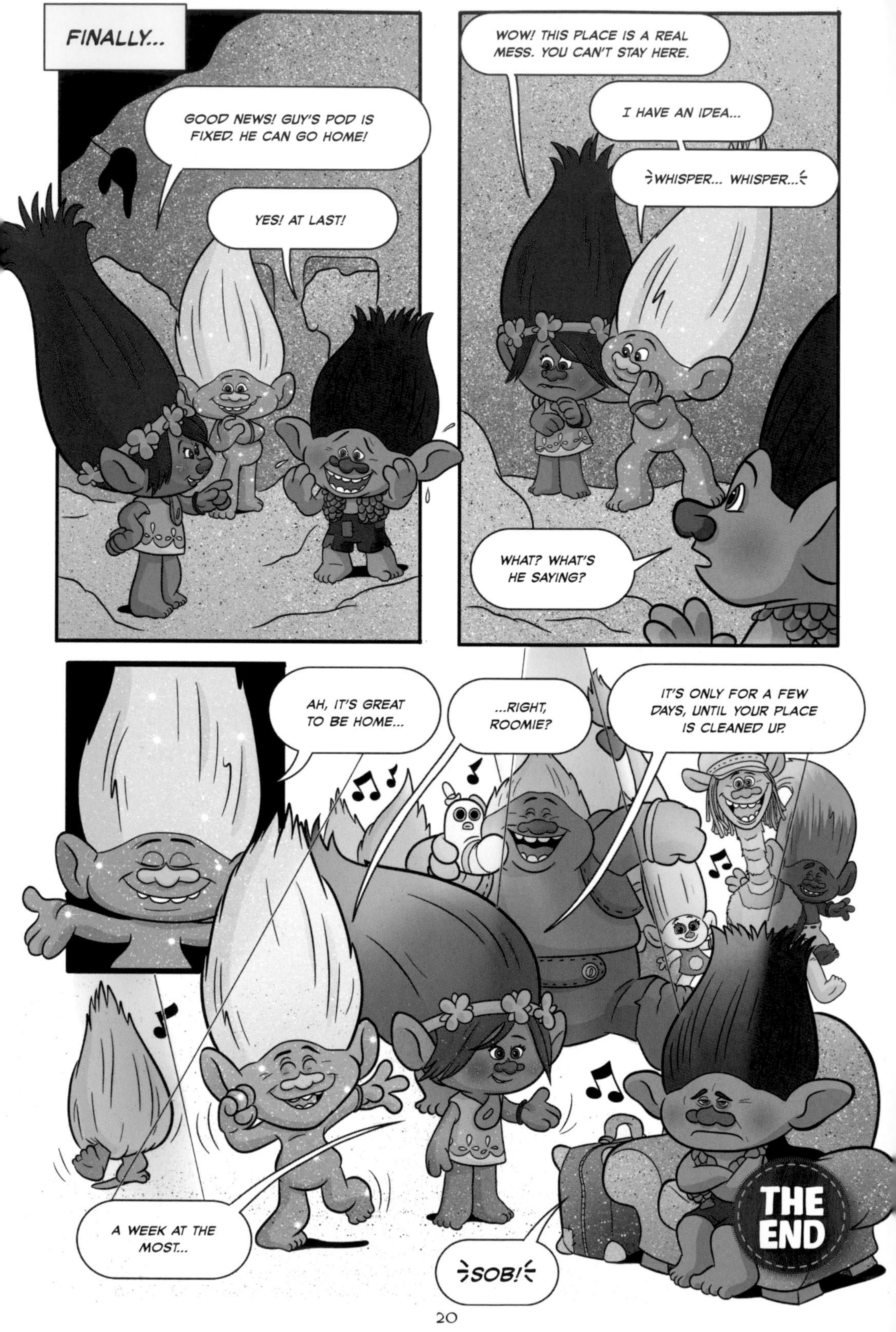
FINALLY...
GOOD NEWS! GUY'S POD IS FIXED. HE CAN GO HOME!
YES! AT LAST!
WOW! THIS PLACE IS A REAL MESS. YOU CAN'T STAY HERE.
I HAVE AN IDEA...
WHISPER... WHISPER...
WHAT? WHAT'S HE SAYING?
AH, IT'S GREAT TO BE HOME...
...RIGHT, ROOMIE?
IT'S ONLY FOR A FEW DAYS, UNTIL YOUR PLACE IS CLEANED UP.
A WEEK AT THE MOST...
SOB!
THE END

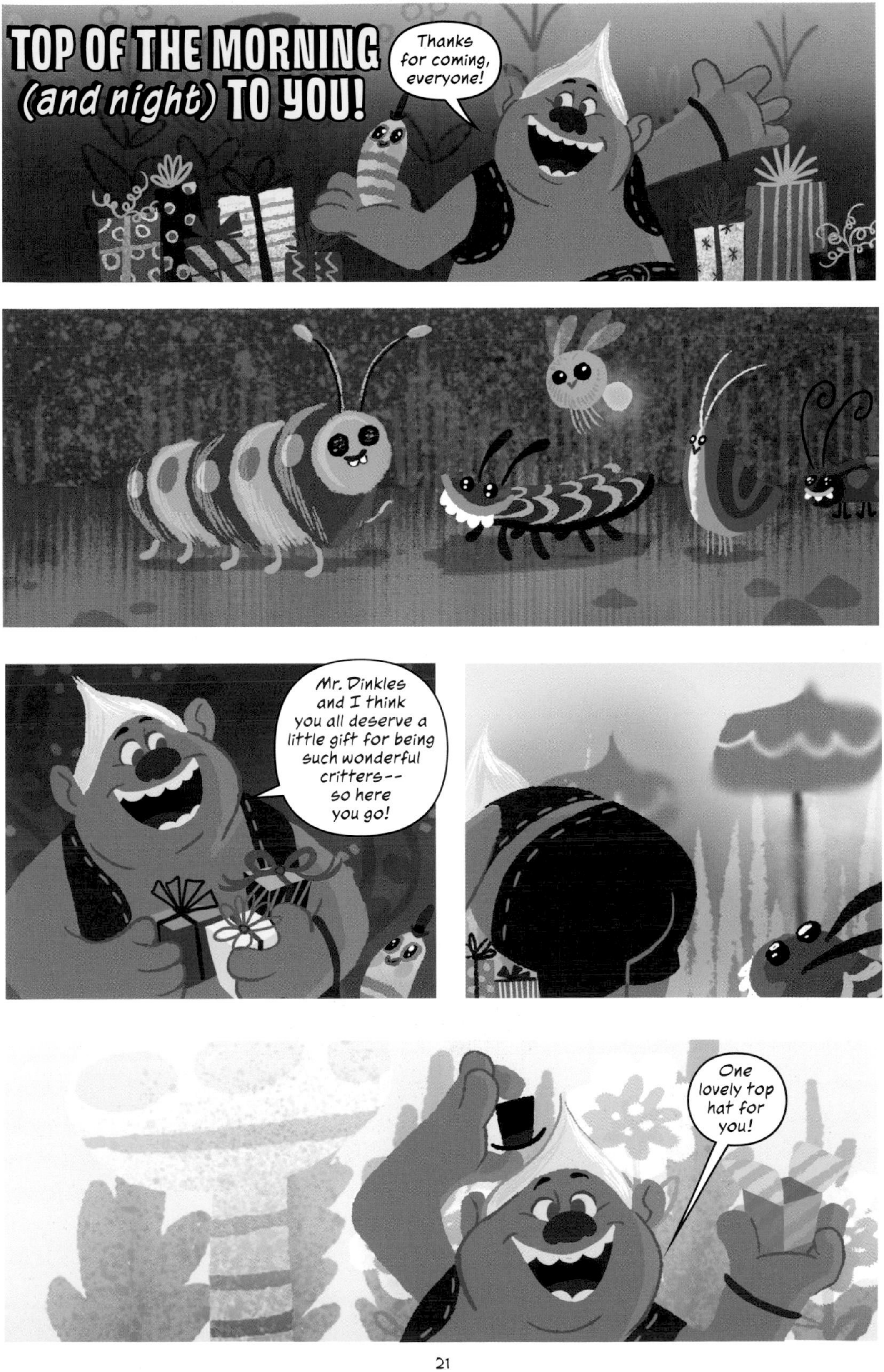
TOP OF THE MORNING (and night) TO YOU!
Thanks for coming, everyone!
Mr. Dinkles and I think you all deserve a little gift for being such wonderful critters-- so here you go!
One lovely top hat for you!

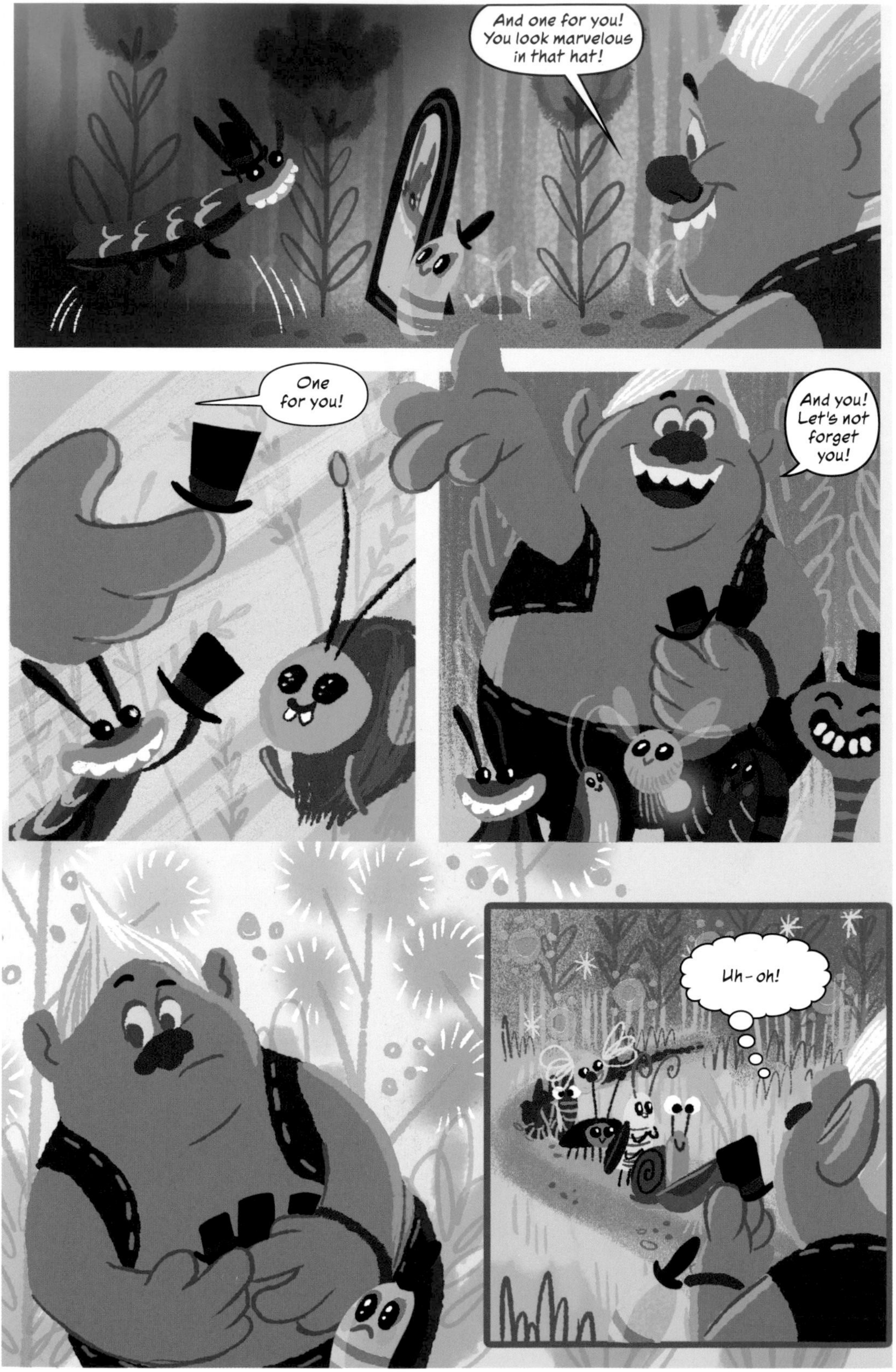
And one for you! You look marvelous in that hat!
One for you!
And you! Let's not forget you!
Uh-oh!

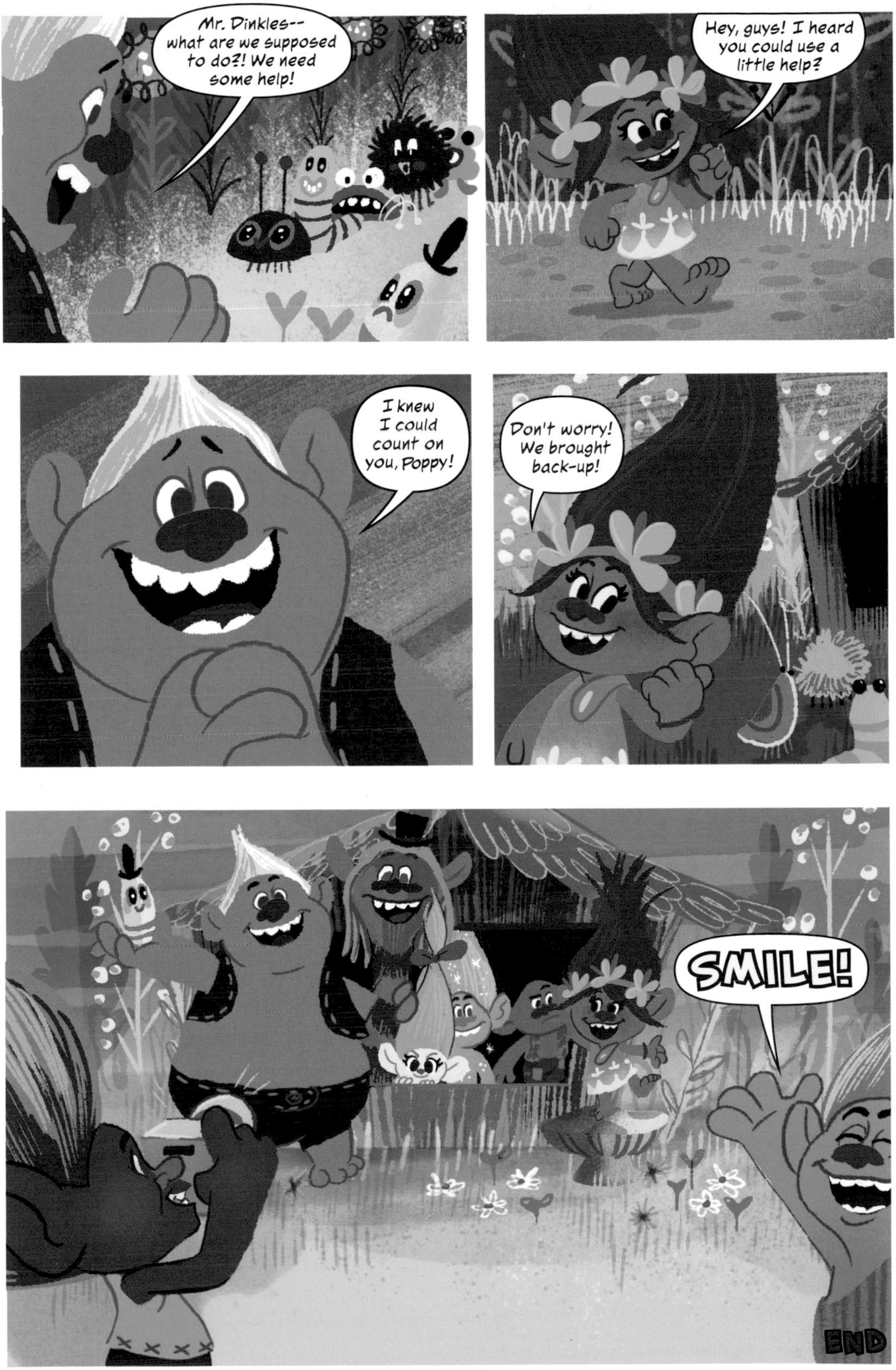
Mr. Dinkles--
what are we supposed
to do?! We need
some help!
Hey, guys! I heard
you could use a
little help?
I knew
I could
count on
you, Poppy!
Don't worry!
We brought
back-up!
SMILE!
END

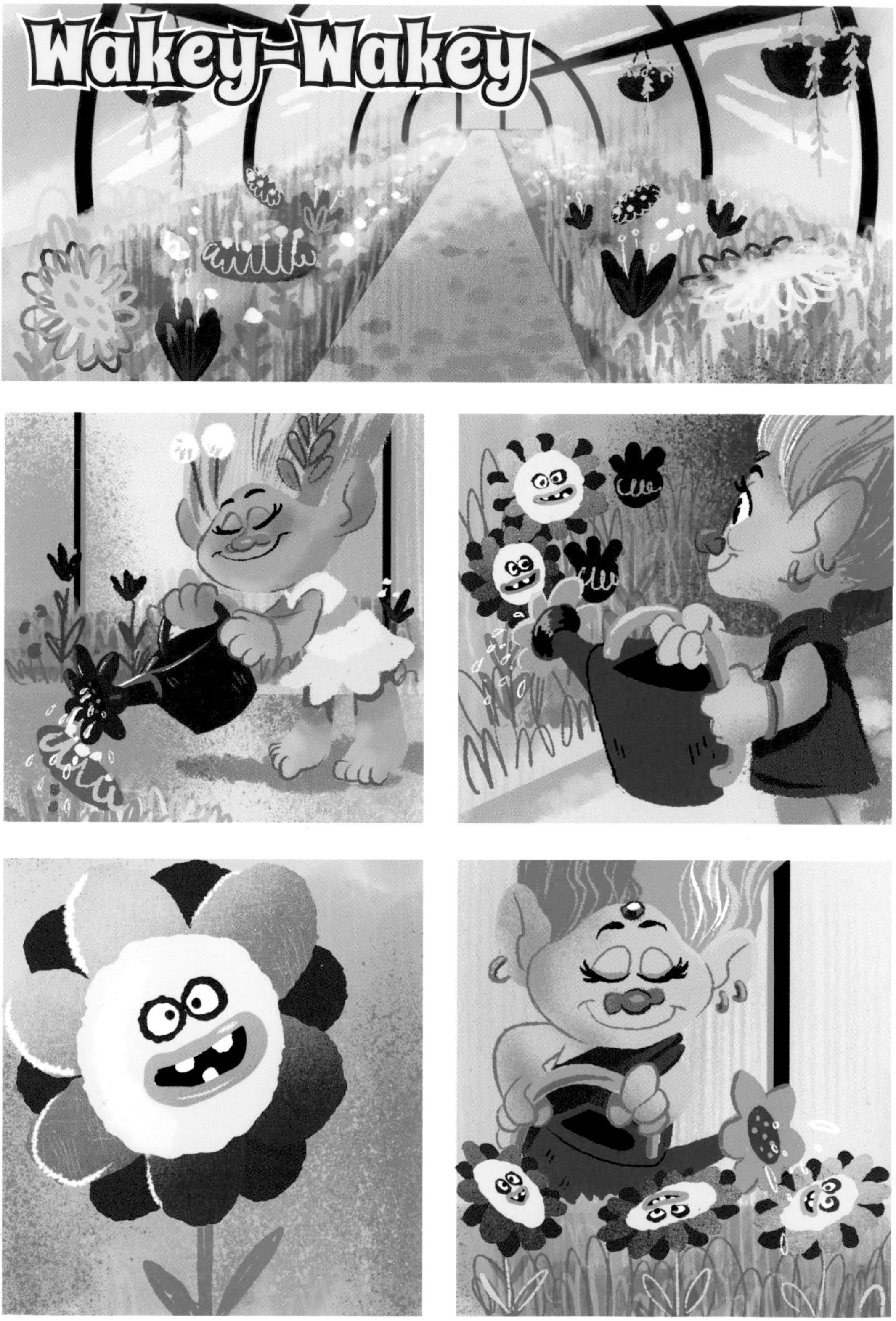
Wakey-Wakey

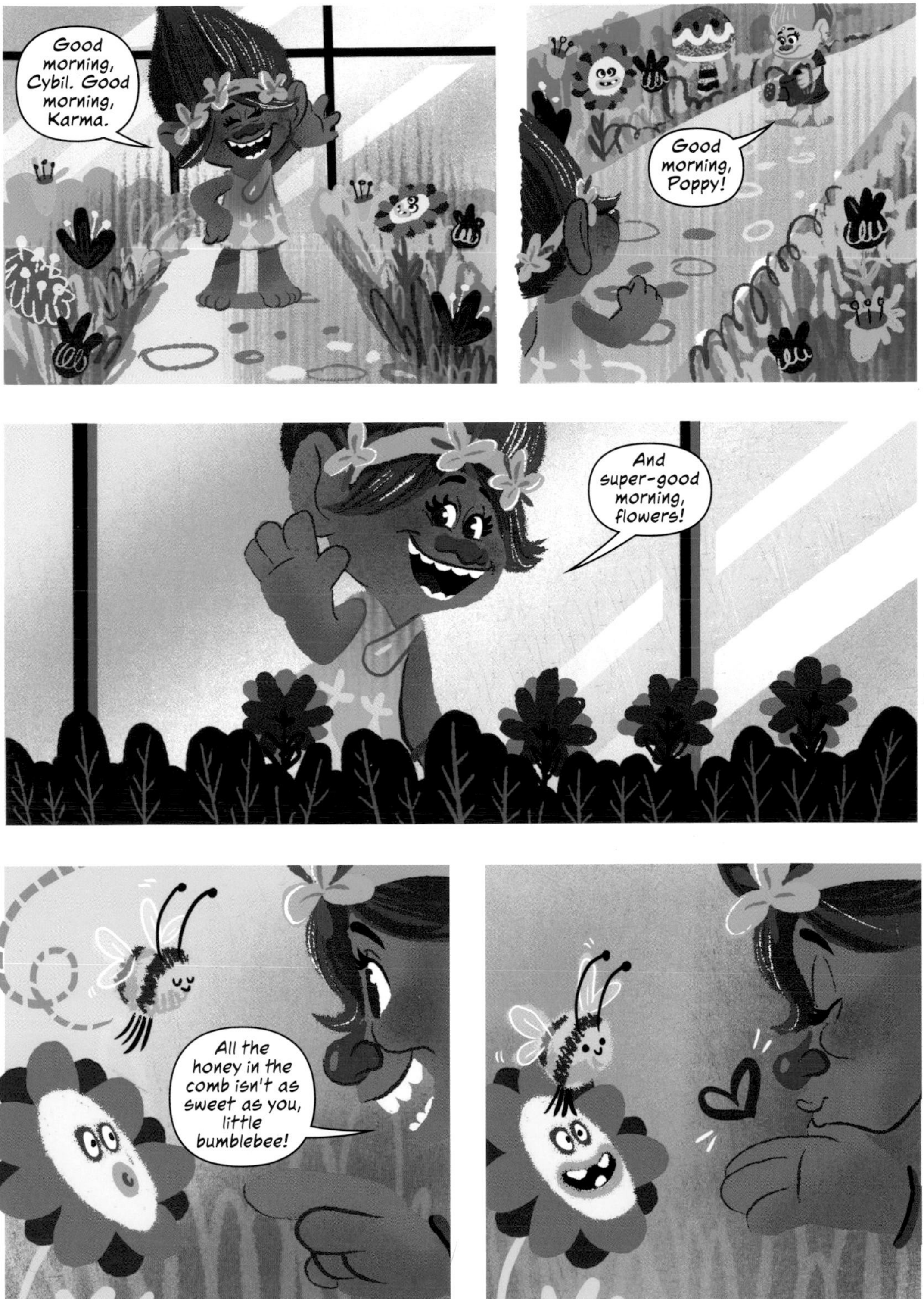
Good morning, Cybil. Good morning, Karma.
Good morning, Poppy!
And super-good morning, flowers!
All the honey in the comb isn't as sweet as you, little bumblebee!

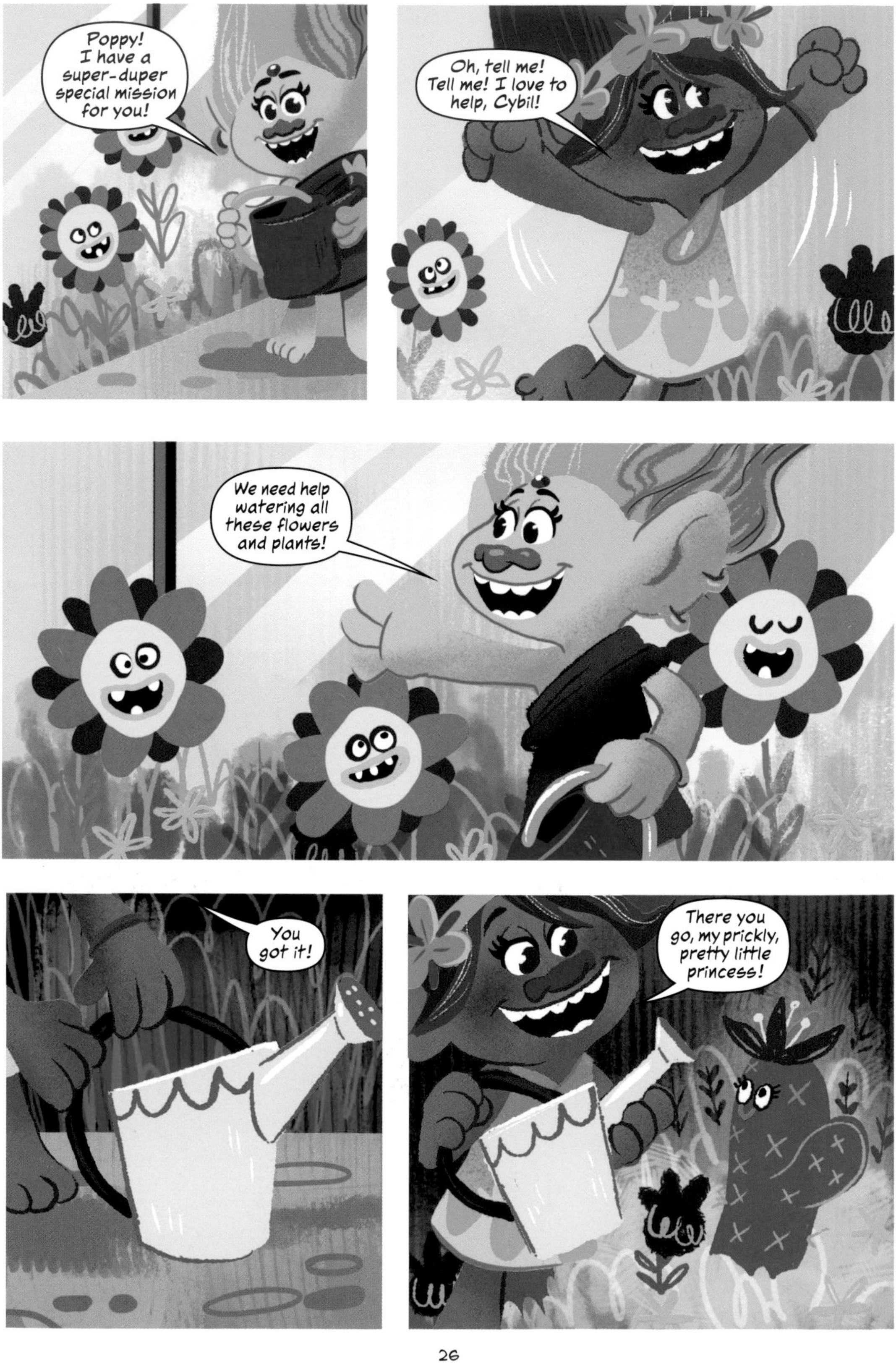
Poppy! I have a super-duper special mission for you!
Oh, tell me! Tell me! I love to help, Cybil!
We need help watering all these flowers and plants!
You got it!
There you go, my prickly, pretty little princess!

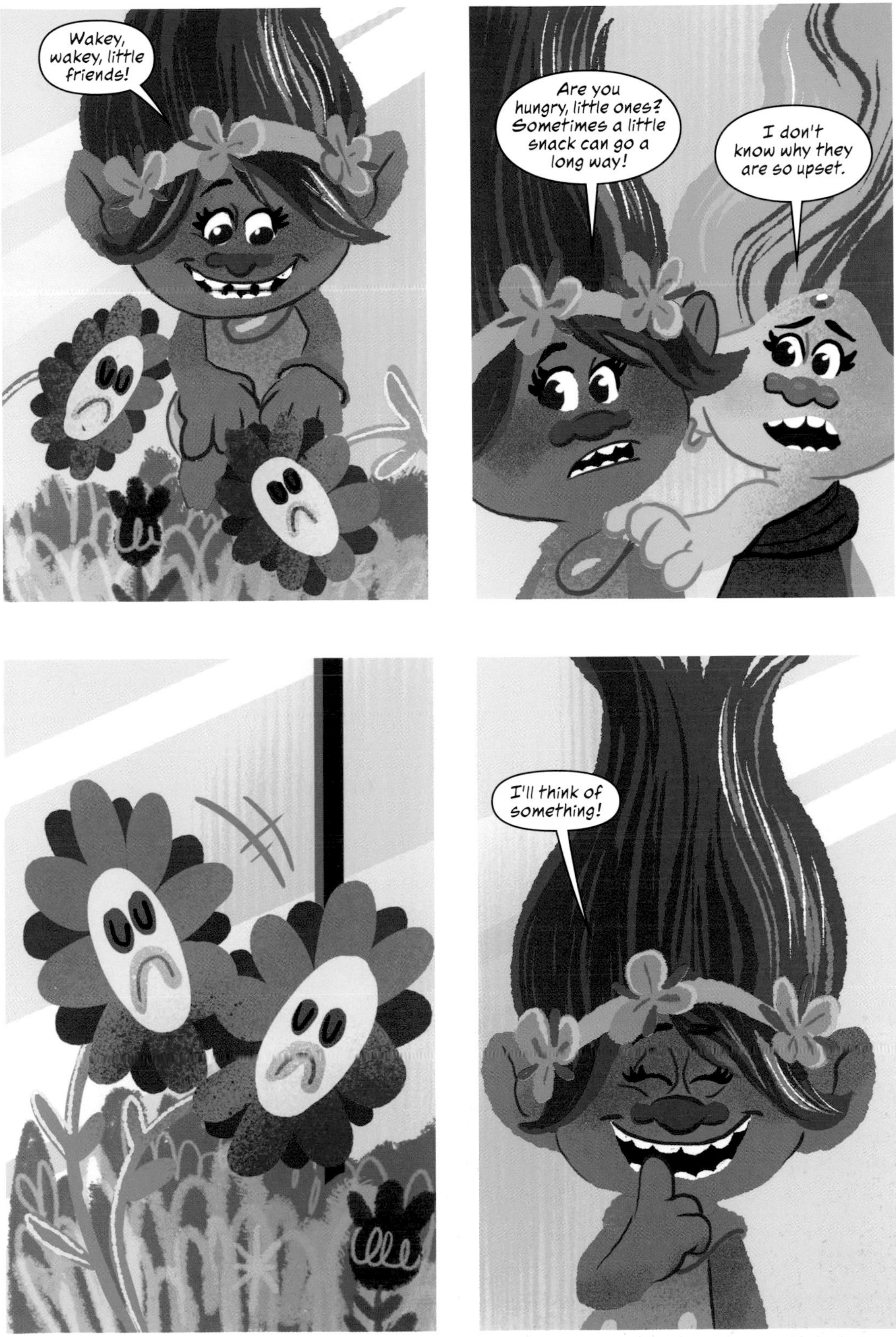
Wakey, wakey, little friends!
Are you hungry, little ones? Sometimes a little snack can go a long way!
I don't know why they are so upset.
I'll think of something!

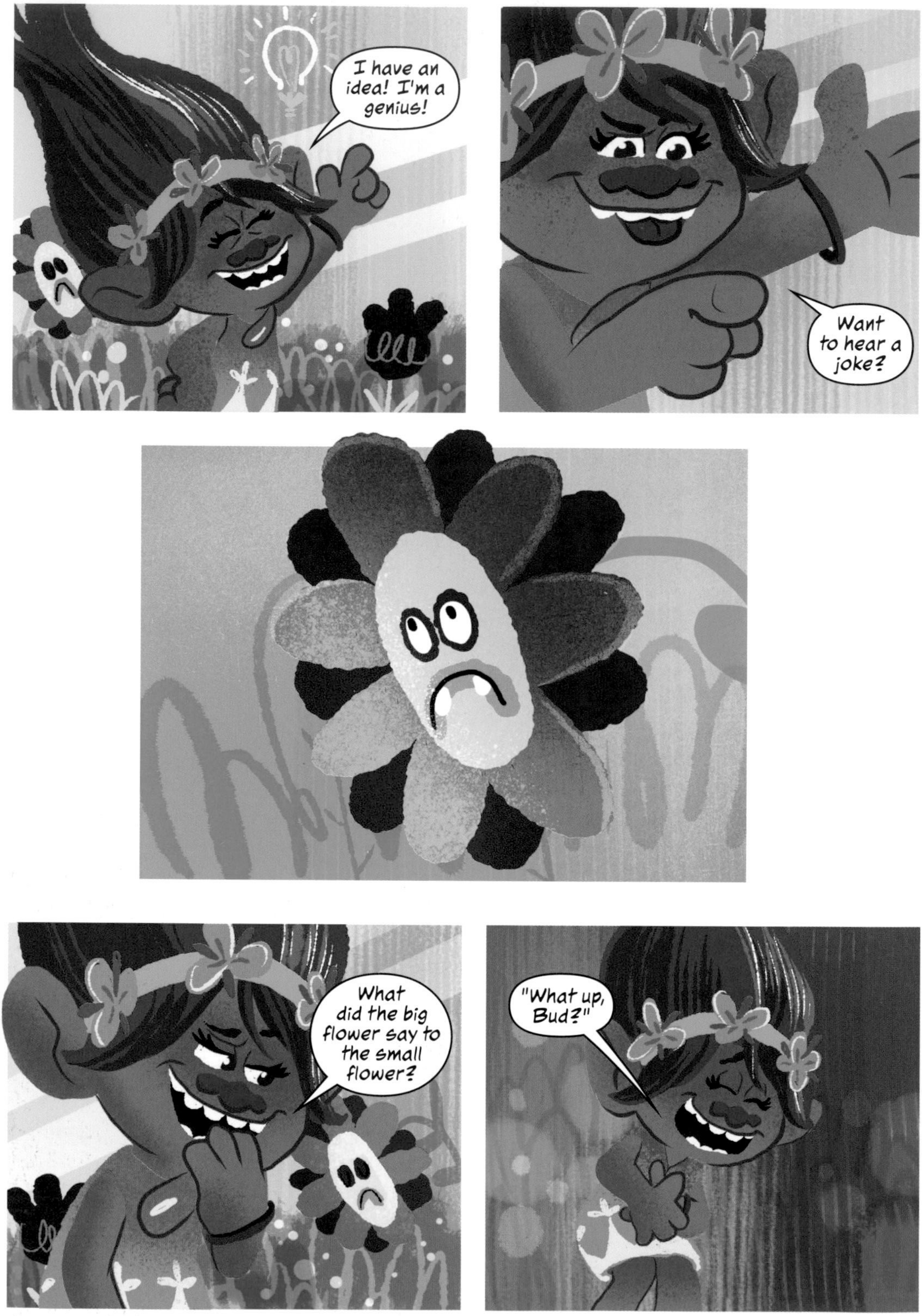
I have an idea! I'm a genius!
Want to hear a joke?
What did the big flower say to the small flower?
"What up, Bud?"

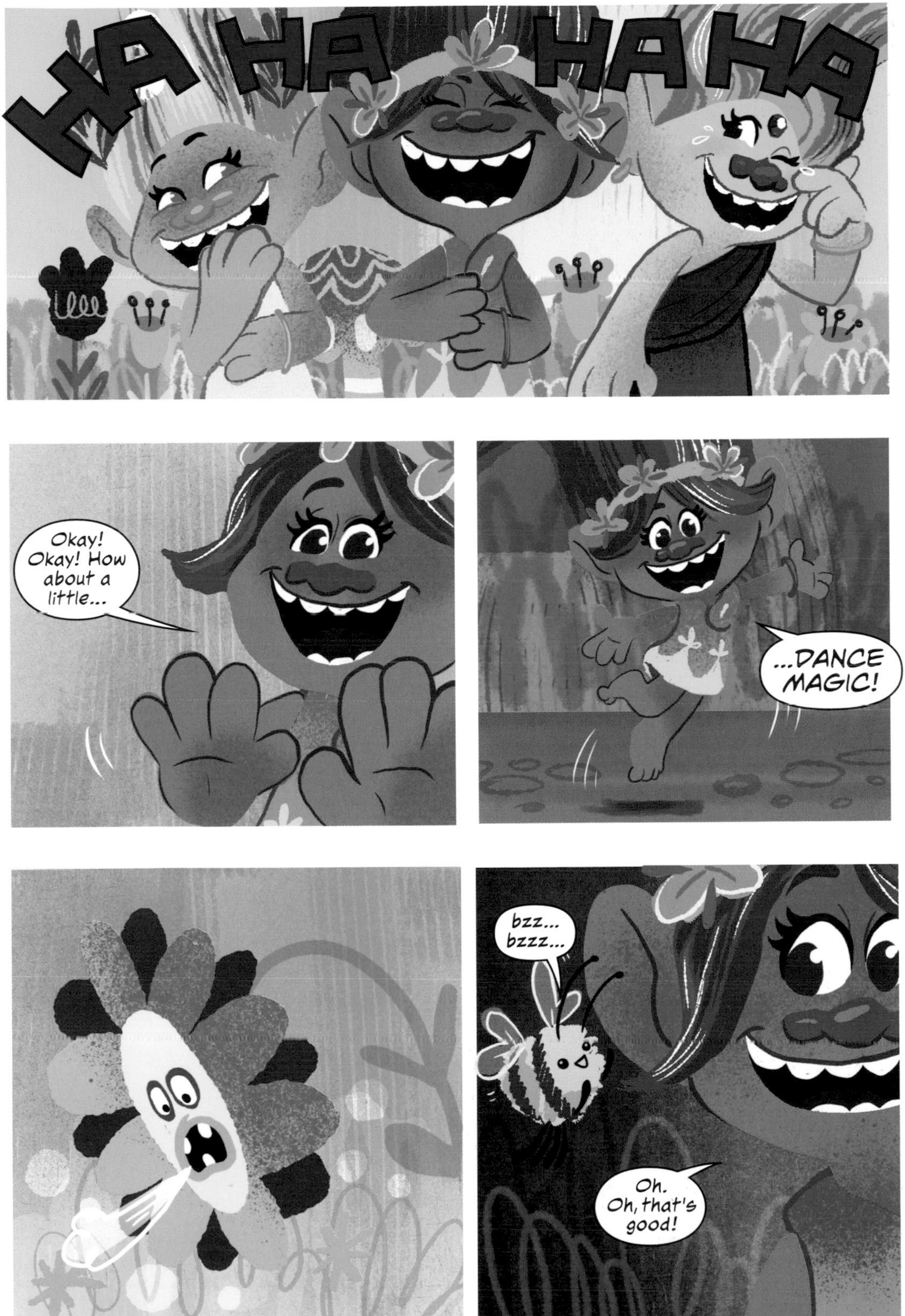
HA HA HA HA HA
Okay! Okay! How about a little...
...DANCE MAGIC!
bzz... bzzz...
Oh. Oh, that's good!

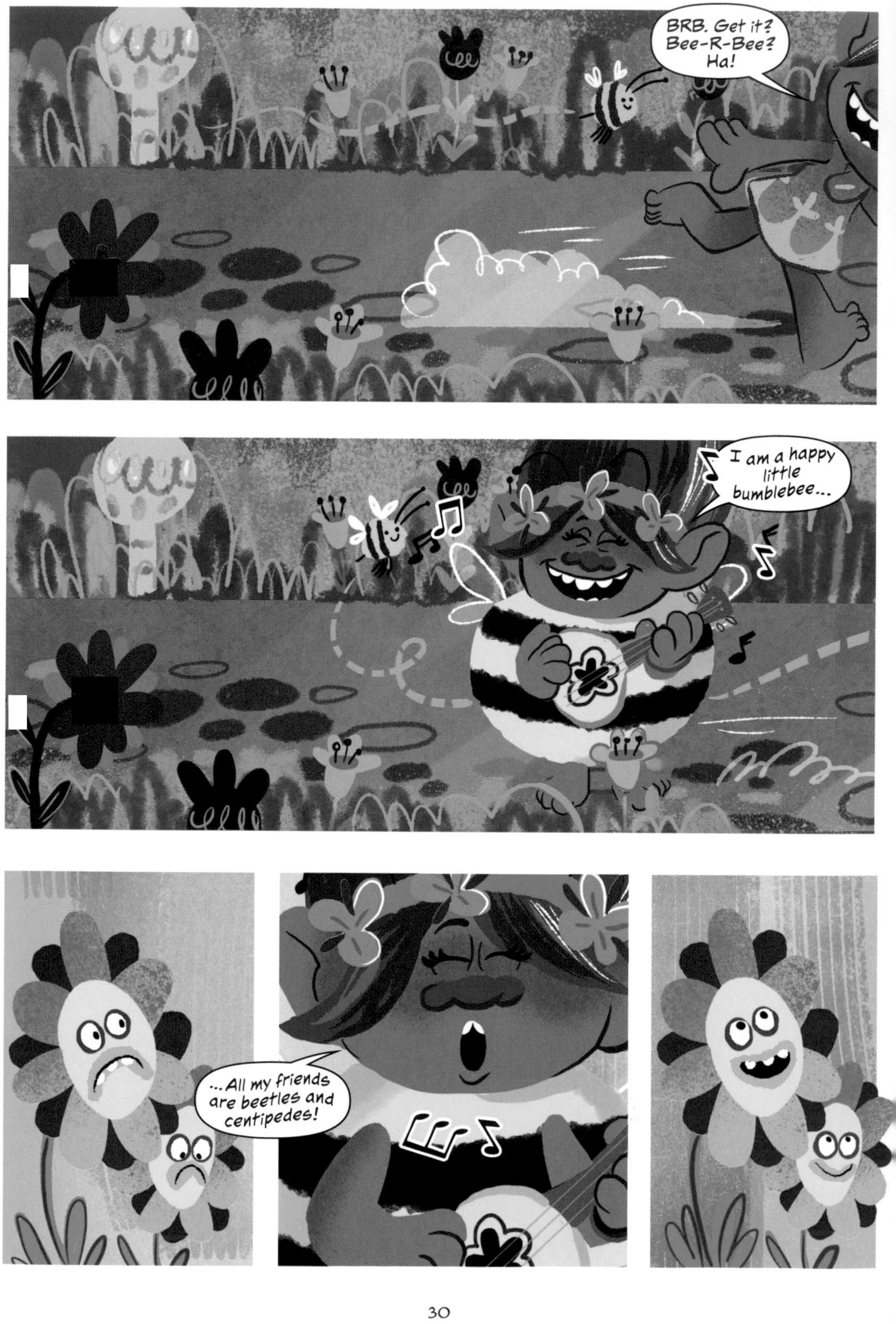
BRB. Get it? Bee-R-Bee? Ha!
I am a happy little bumblebee...
...All my friends are beetles and centipedes!

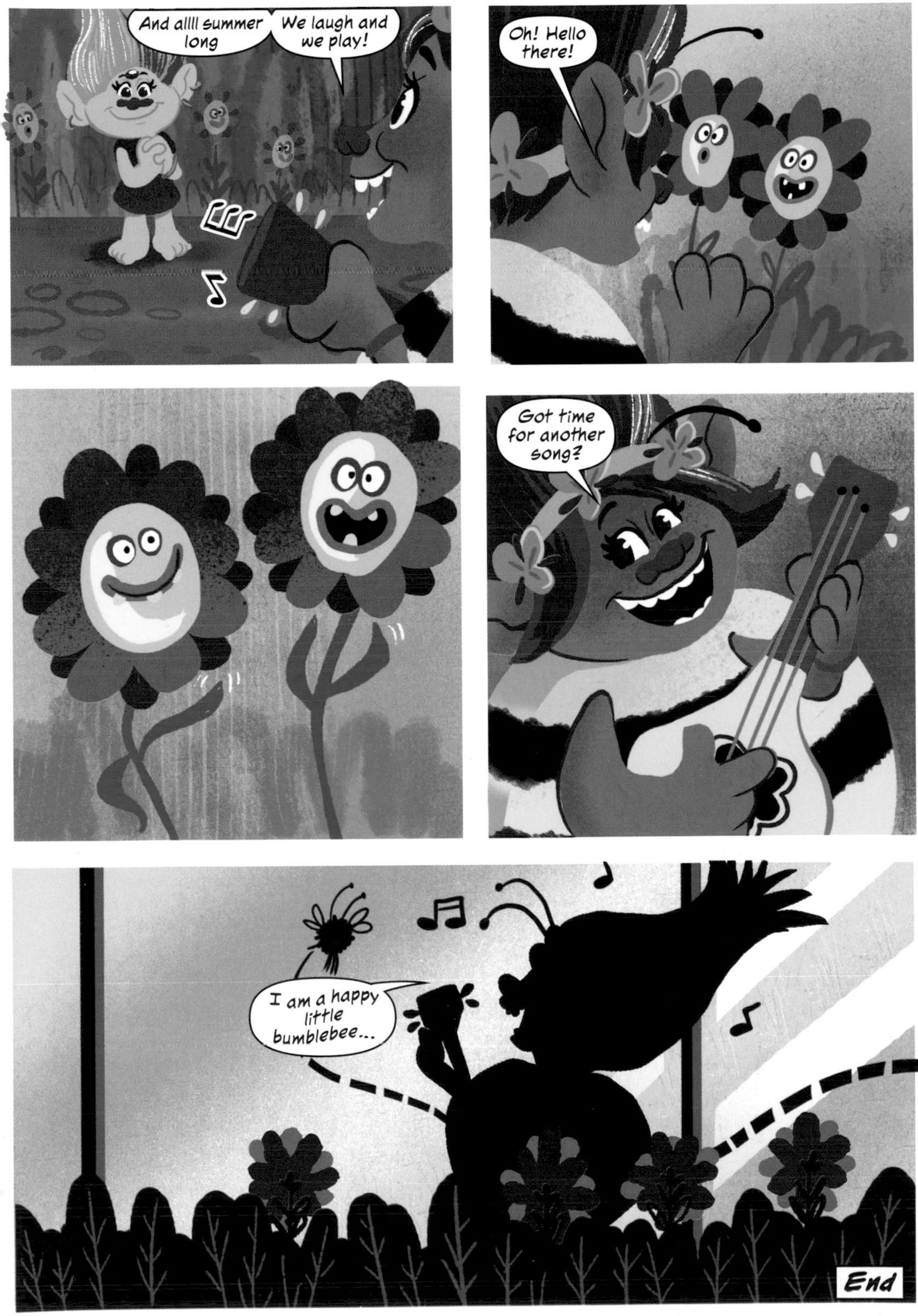
And allll summer long
We laugh and we play!
Oh! Hello there!
Got time for another song?
I am a happy little bumblebee...
End

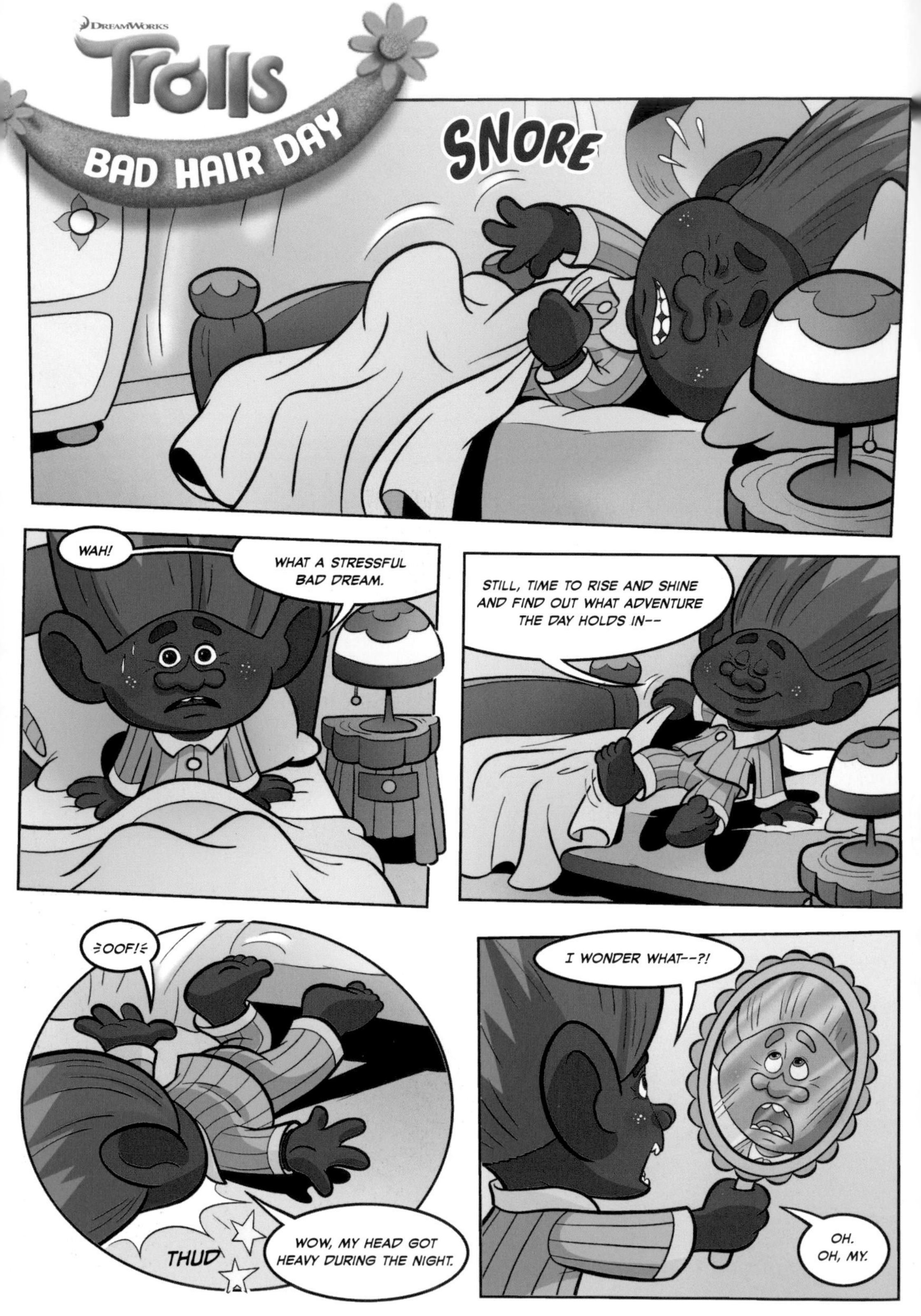
DreamWorks
Trolls
BAD HAIR DAY
SNORE
WAH!
WHAT A STRESSFUL BAD DREAM.
STILL, TIME TO RISE AND SHINE AND FIND OUT WHAT ADVENTURE THE DAY HOLDS IN--
OOF!
THUD
WOW, MY HEAD GOT HEAVY DURING THE NIGHT.
I WONDER WHAT--?!
OH. OH, MY.

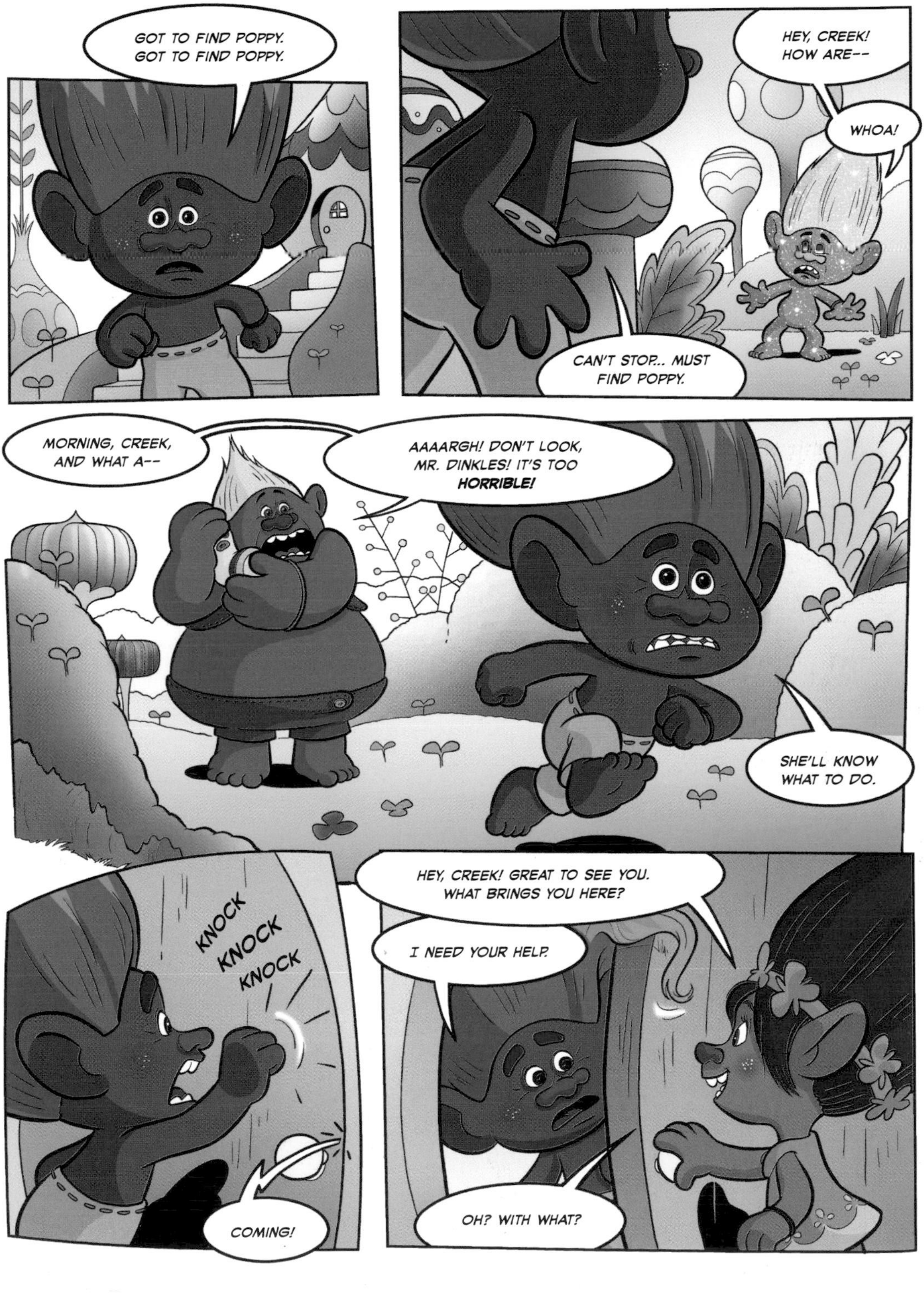
GOT TO FIND POPPY. GOT TO FIND POPPY.
HEY, CREEK! HOW ARE--
WHOA!
CAN'T STOP... MUST FIND POPPY.
MORNING, CREEK, AND WHAT A--
AAAARGH! DON'T LOOK, MR. DINKLES! IT'S TOO HORRIBLE!
SHE'LL KNOW WHAT TO DO.
KNOCK KNOCK KNOCK
COMING!
HEY, CREEK! GREAT TO SEE YOU. WHAT BRINGS YOU HERE?
I NEED YOUR HELP.
OH? WITH WHAT?

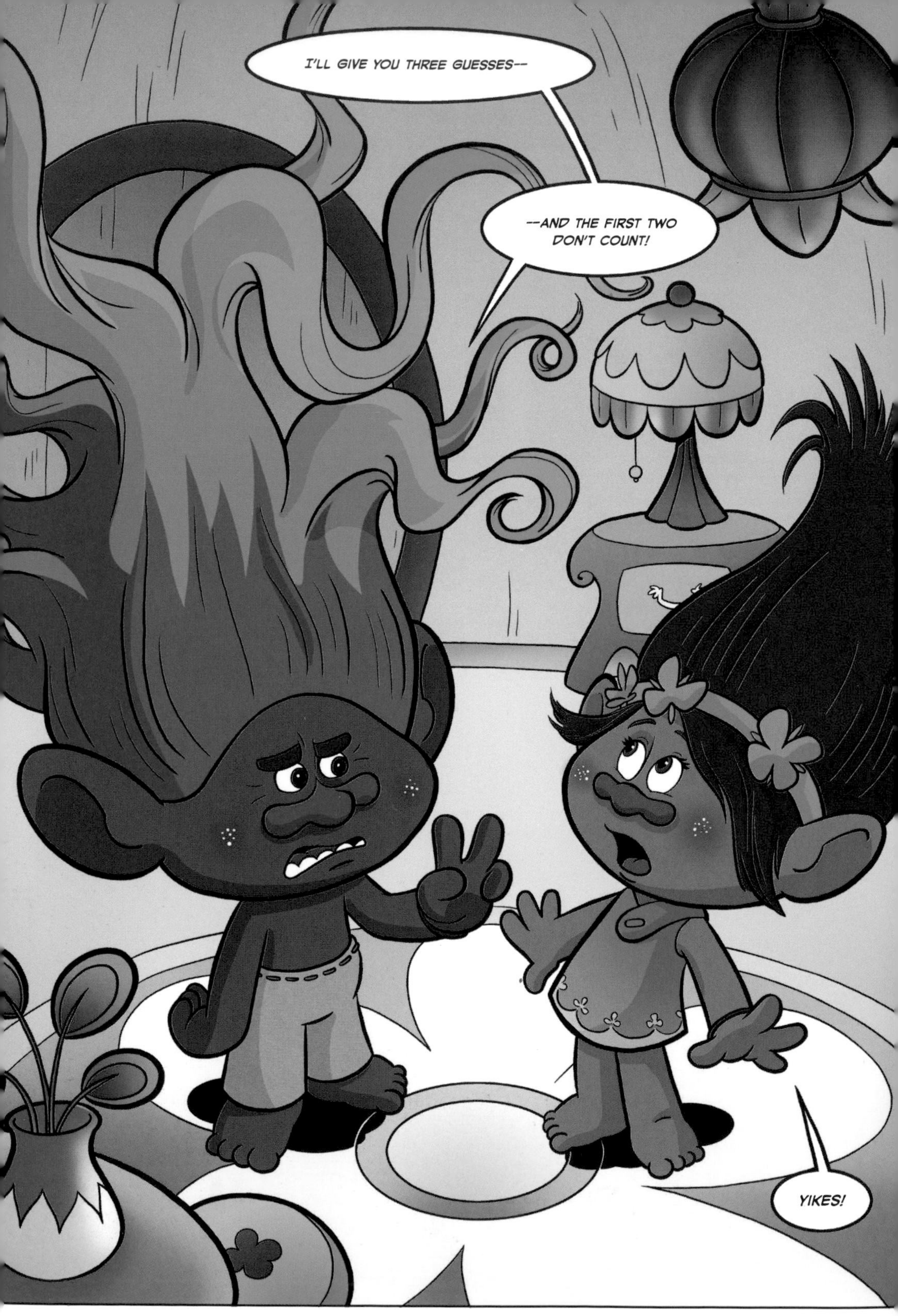
I'LL GIVE YOU THREE GUESSES--
--AND THE FIRST TWO DON'T COUNT!
YIKES!

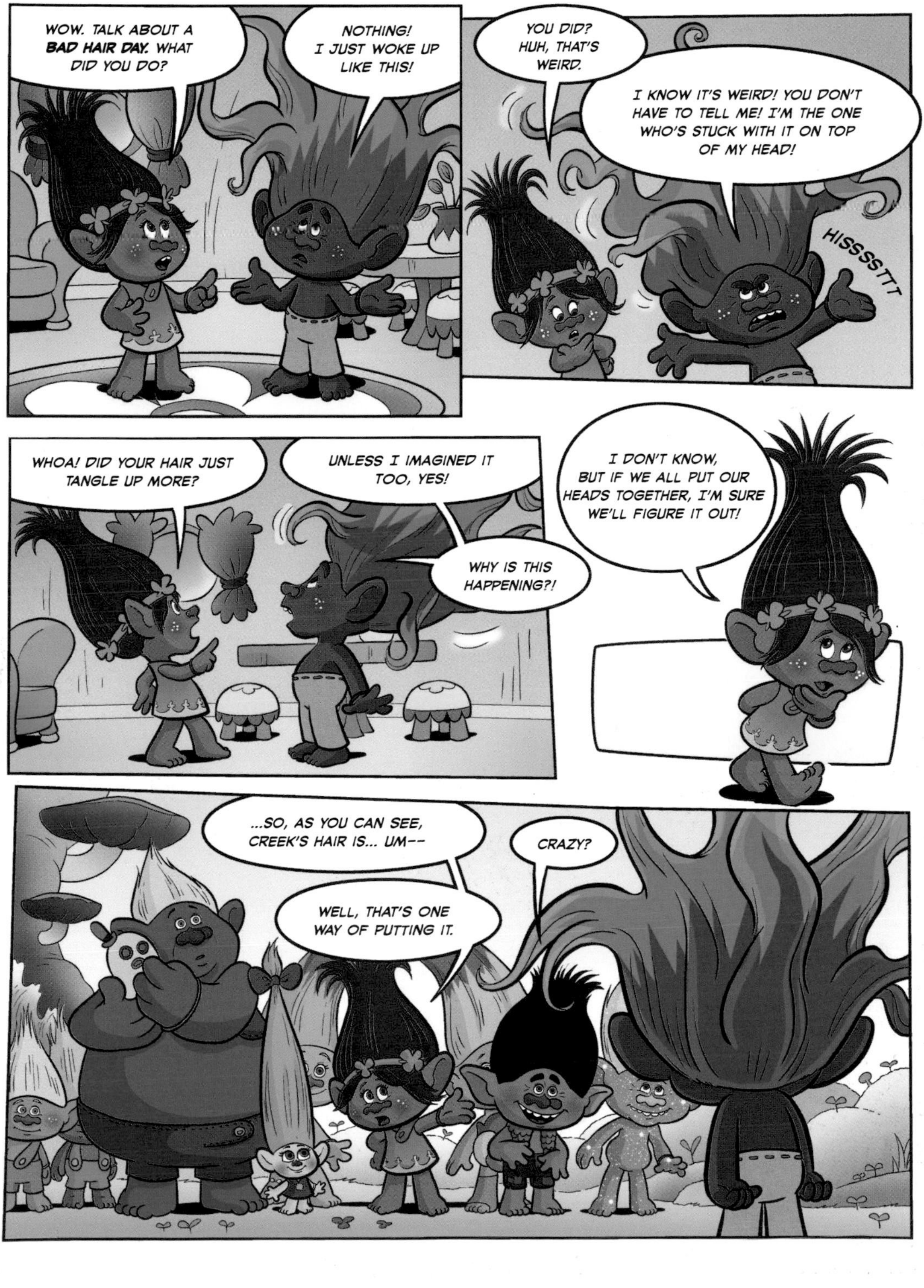
WOW. TALK ABOUT A **BAD HAIR DAY.** WHAT DID YOU DO?
NOTHING! I JUST WOKE UP LIKE THIS!
YOU DID? HUH, THAT'S WEIRD.
I KNOW IT'S WEIRD! YOU DON'T HAVE TO TELL ME! I'M THE ONE WHO'S STUCK WITH IT ON TOP OF MY HEAD!
HISSSSTTT
WHOA! DID YOUR HAIR JUST TANGLE UP MORE?
UNLESS I IMAGINED IT TOO, YES!
WHY IS THIS HAPPENING?!
I DON'T KNOW, BUT IF WE ALL PUT OUR HEADS TOGETHER, I'M SURE WE'LL FIGURE IT OUT!
...SO, AS YOU CAN SEE, CREEK'S HAIR IS... UM--
CRAZY?
WELL, THAT'S ONE WAY OF PUTTING IT.

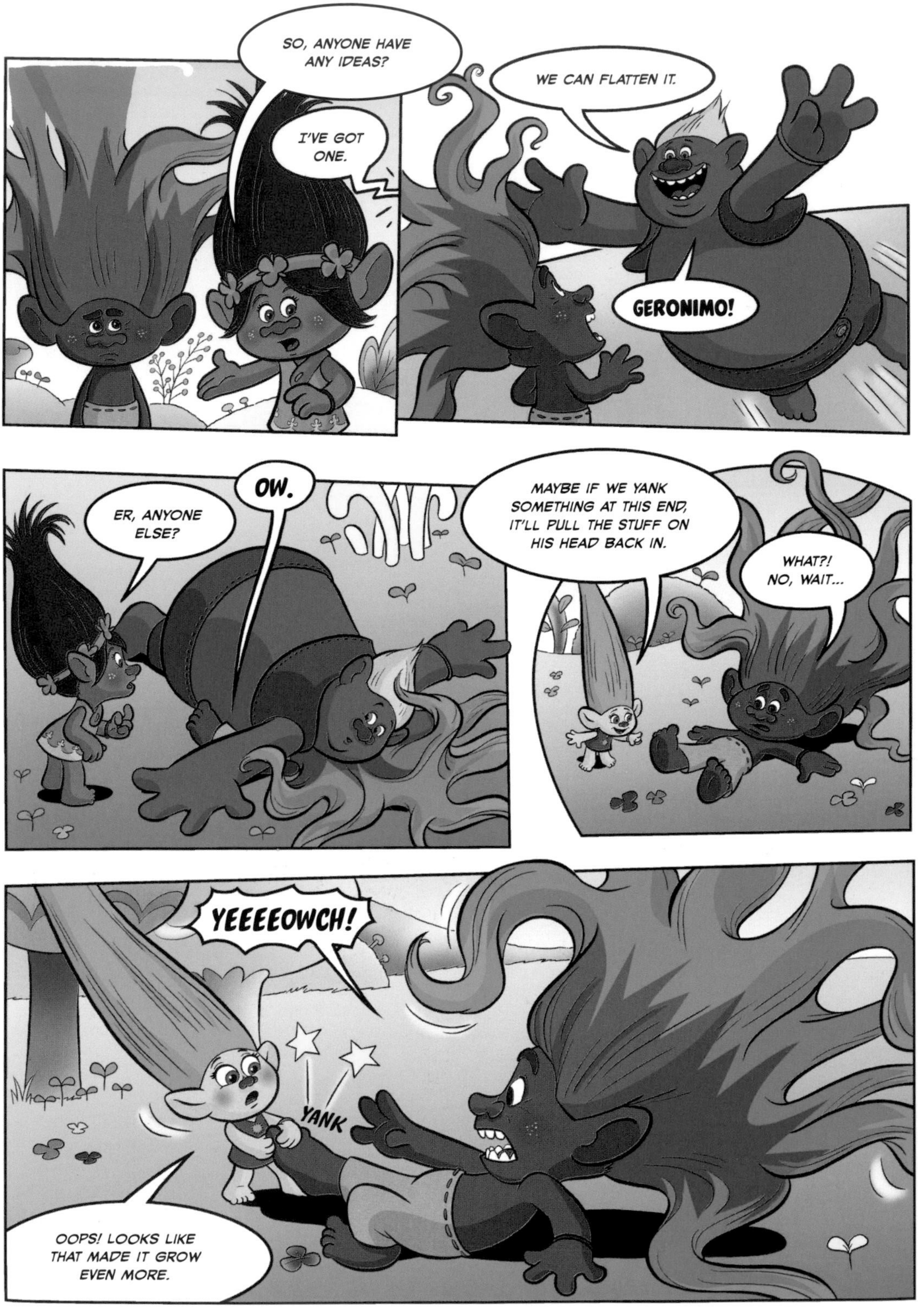
SO, ANYONE HAVE ANY IDEAS?
I'VE GOT ONE.
WE CAN FLATTEN IT.
GERONIMO!
ER, ANYONE ELSE?
OW.
MAYBE IF WE YANK SOMETHING AT THIS END, IT'LL PULL THE STUFF ON HIS HEAD BACK IN.
WHAT?! NO, WAIT...
YEEEEOWCH!
YANK
OOPS! LOOKS LIKE THAT MADE IT GROW EVEN MORE.

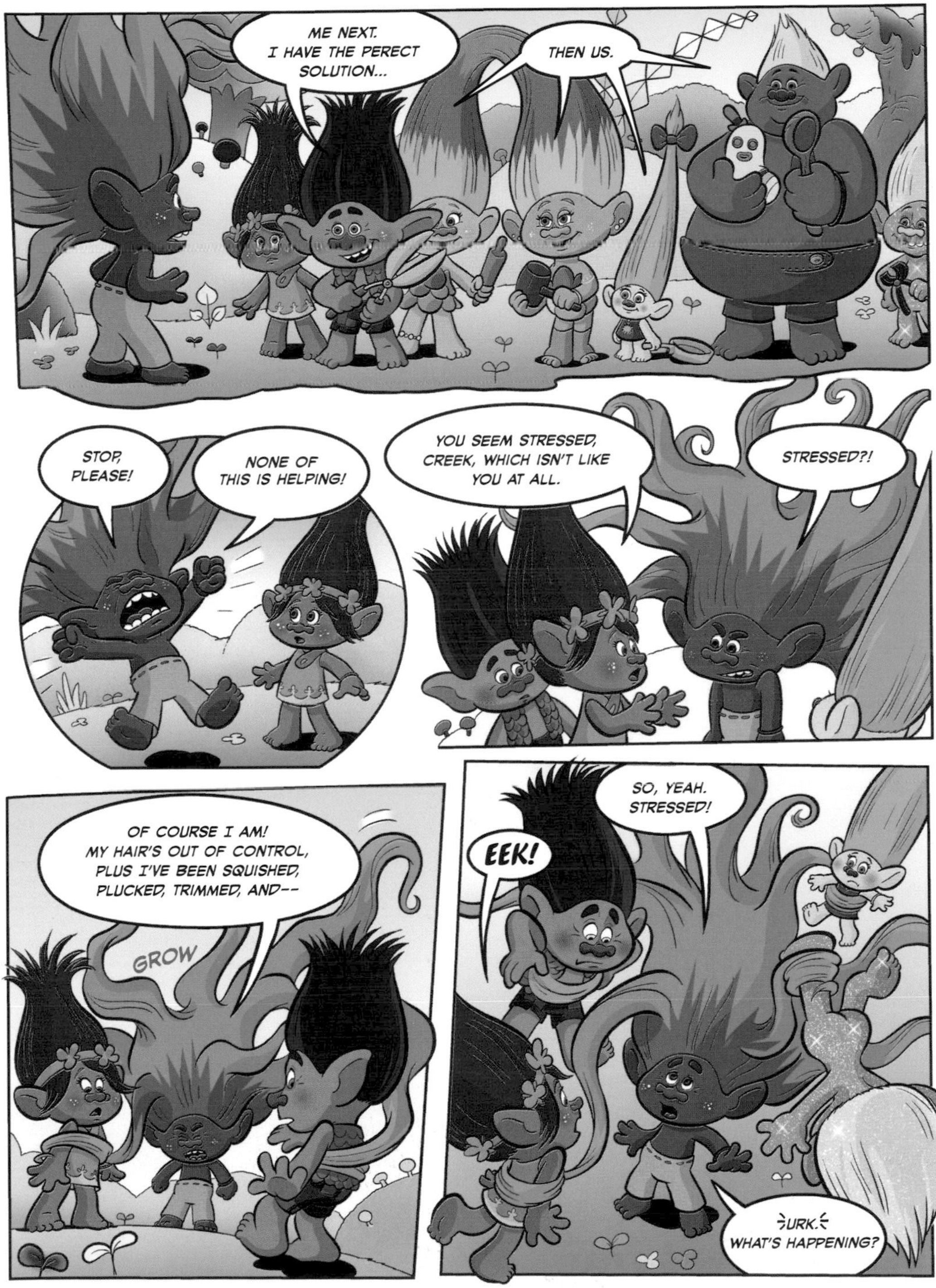
ME NEXT. I HAVE THE PERECT SOLUTION...
THEN US.
STOP, PLEASE!
NONE OF THIS IS HELPING!
YOU SEEM STRESSED, CREEK, WHICH ISN'T LIKE YOU AT ALL.
STRESSED?!
OF COURSE I AM! MY HAIR'S OUT OF CONTROL, PLUS I'VE BEEN SQUISHED, PLUCKED, TRIMMED, AND--
GROW
EEK!
SO, YEAH. STRESSED!
URK. WHAT'S HAPPENING?

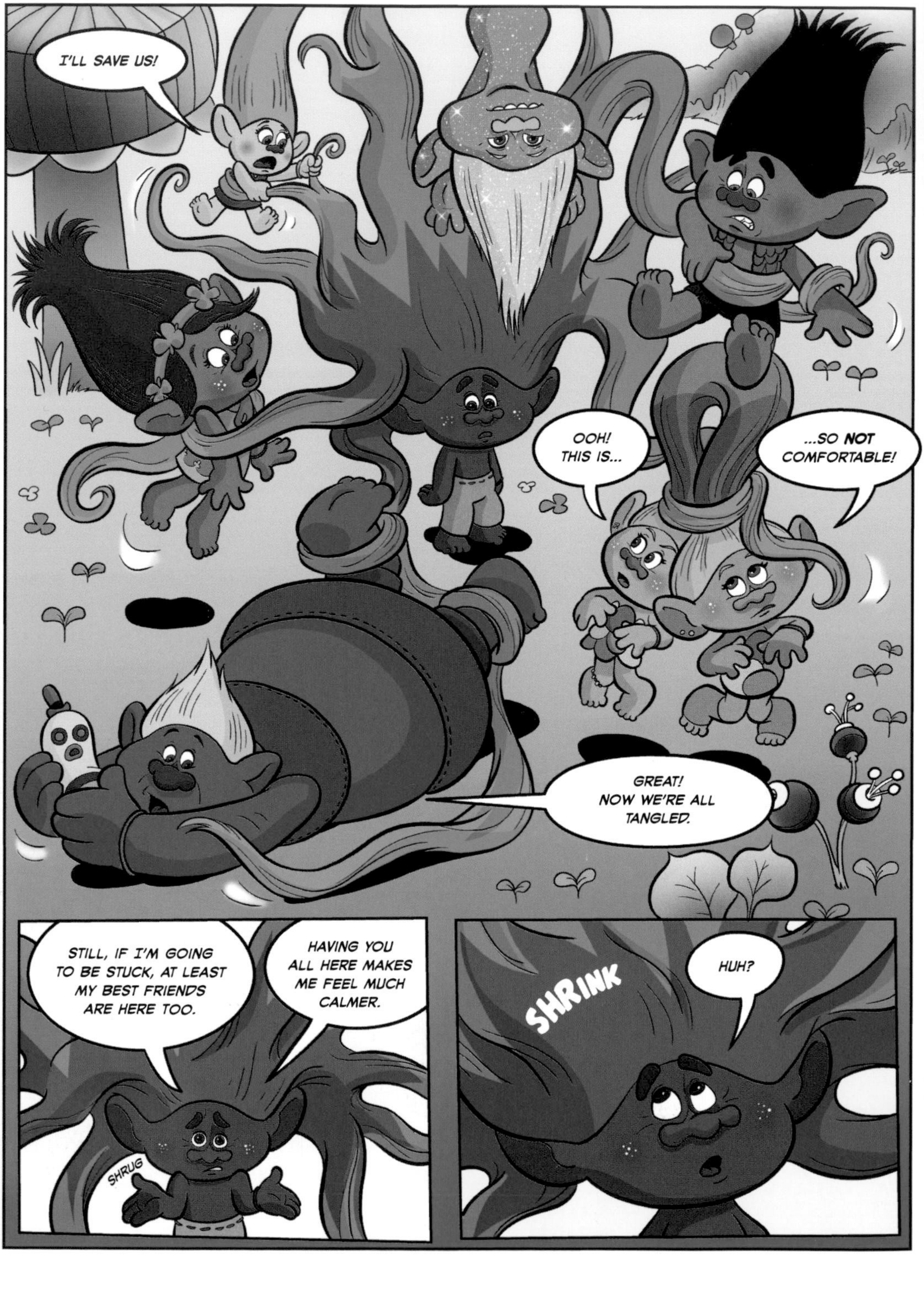
I'LL SAVE US!
OOH! THIS IS...
...SO NOT COMFORTABLE!
GREAT! NOW WE'RE ALL TANGLED.
STILL, IF I'M GOING TO BE STUCK, AT LEAST MY BEST FRIENDS ARE HERE TOO.
HAVING YOU ALL HERE MAKES ME FEEL MUCH CALMER.
SHRUG
SHRINK
HUH?

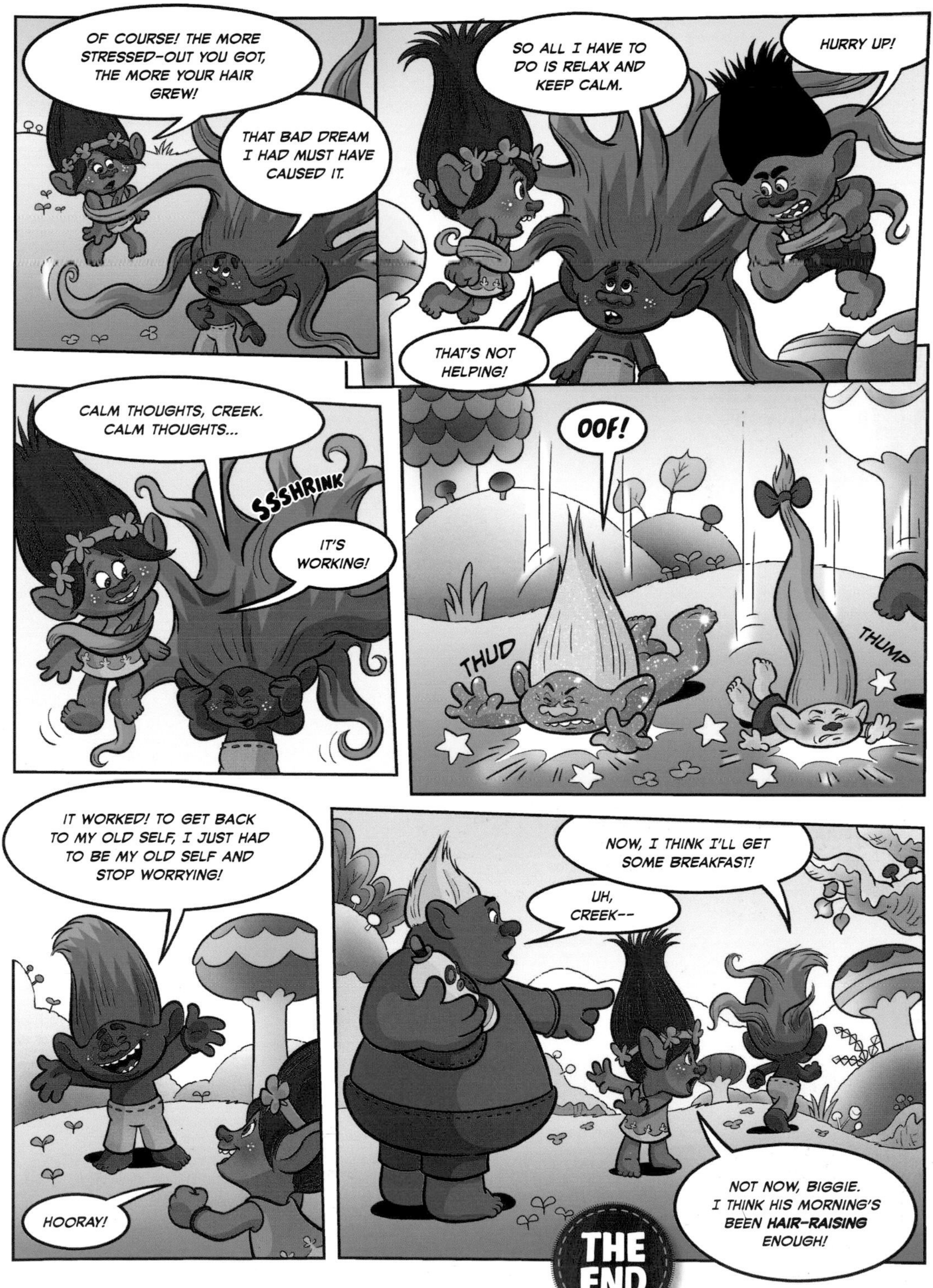
OF COURSE! THE MORE STRESSED-OUT YOU GOT, THE MORE YOUR HAIR GREW!
THAT BAD DREAM I HAD MUST HAVE CAUSED IT.
SO ALL I HAVE TO DO IS RELAX AND KEEP CALM.
HURRY UP!
THAT'S NOT HELPING!
CALM THOUGHTS, CREEK. CALM THOUGHTS...
SSSHRINK
IT'S WORKING!
OOF!
THUD
THUMP
IT WORKED! TO GET BACK TO MY OLD SELF, I JUST HAD TO BE MY OLD SELF AND STOP WORRYING!
HOORAY!
NOW, I THINK I'LL GET SOME BREAKFAST!
UH, CREEK--
NOT NOW, BIGGIE. I THINK HIS MORNING'S BEEN HAIR-RAISING ENOUGH!
THE END

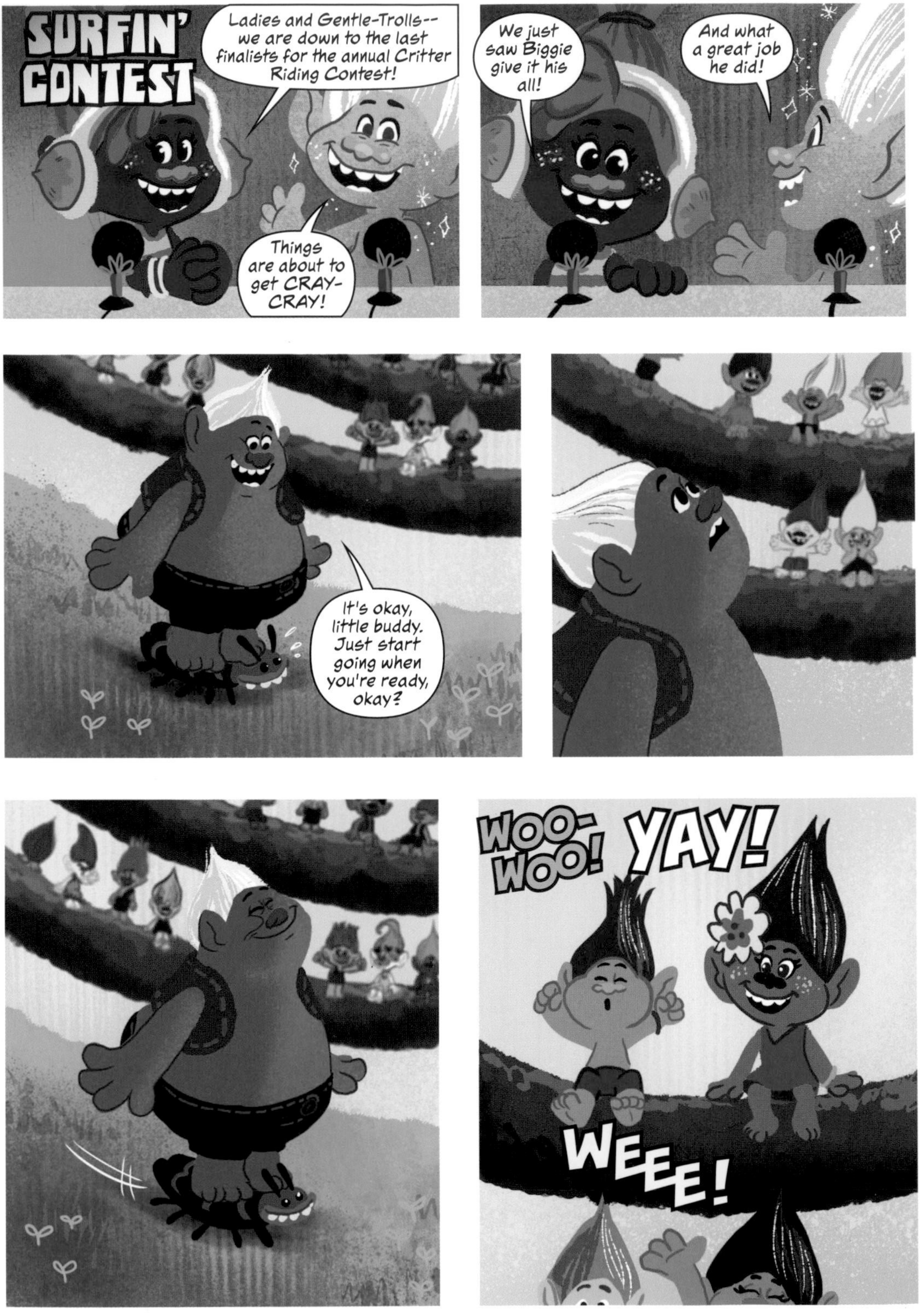
SURFIN' CONTEST
Ladies and Gentle-Trolls-- we are down to the last finalists for the annual Critter Riding Contest!
Things are about to get CRAY-CRAY!
We just saw Biggie give it his all!
And what a great job he did!
It's okay, little buddy. Just start going when you're ready, okay?
WOO-WOO!
YAY!
WEEE!

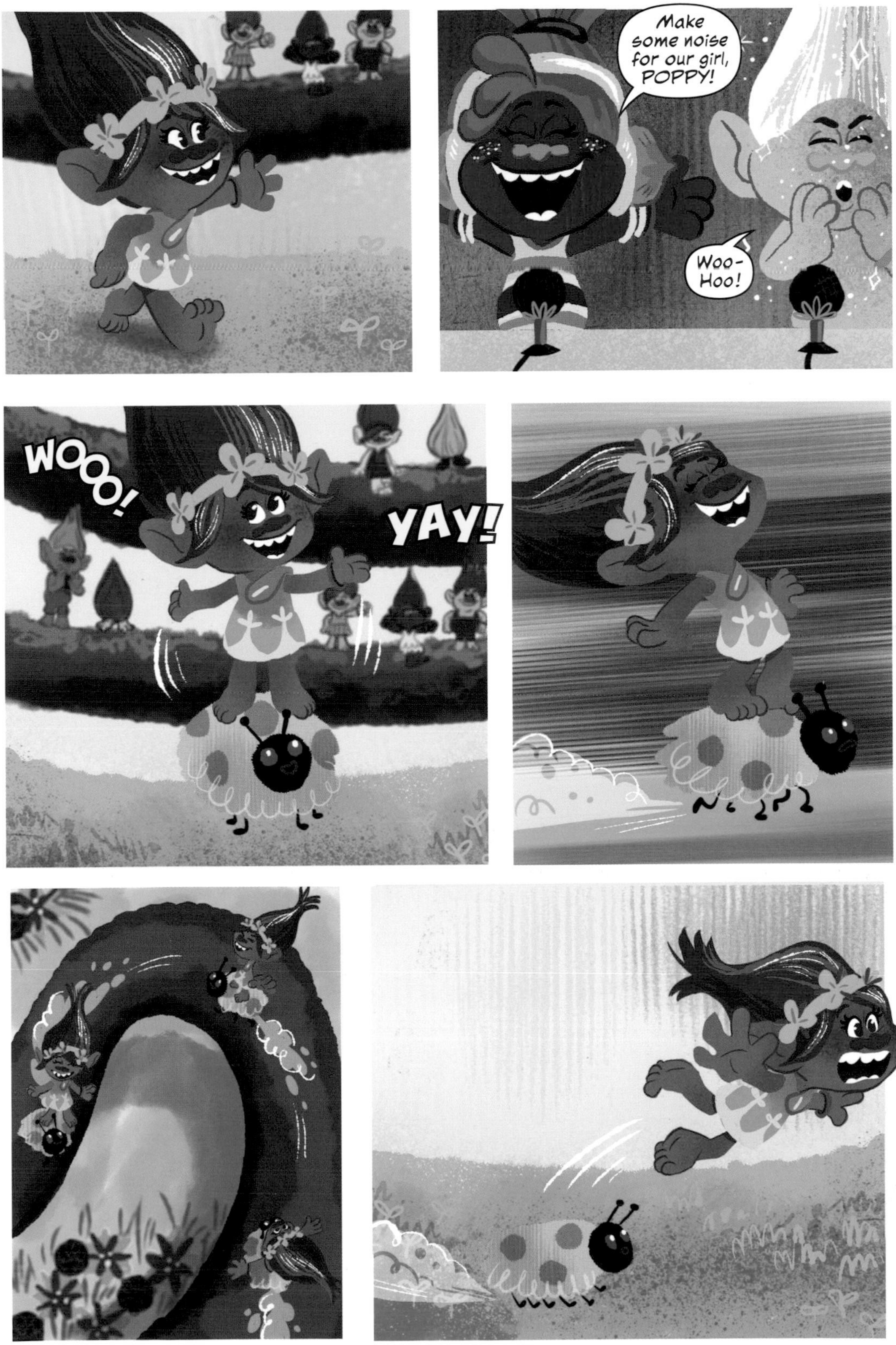
Make some noise for our girl, POPPY!
Woo-Hoo!
WOOO!
YAY!

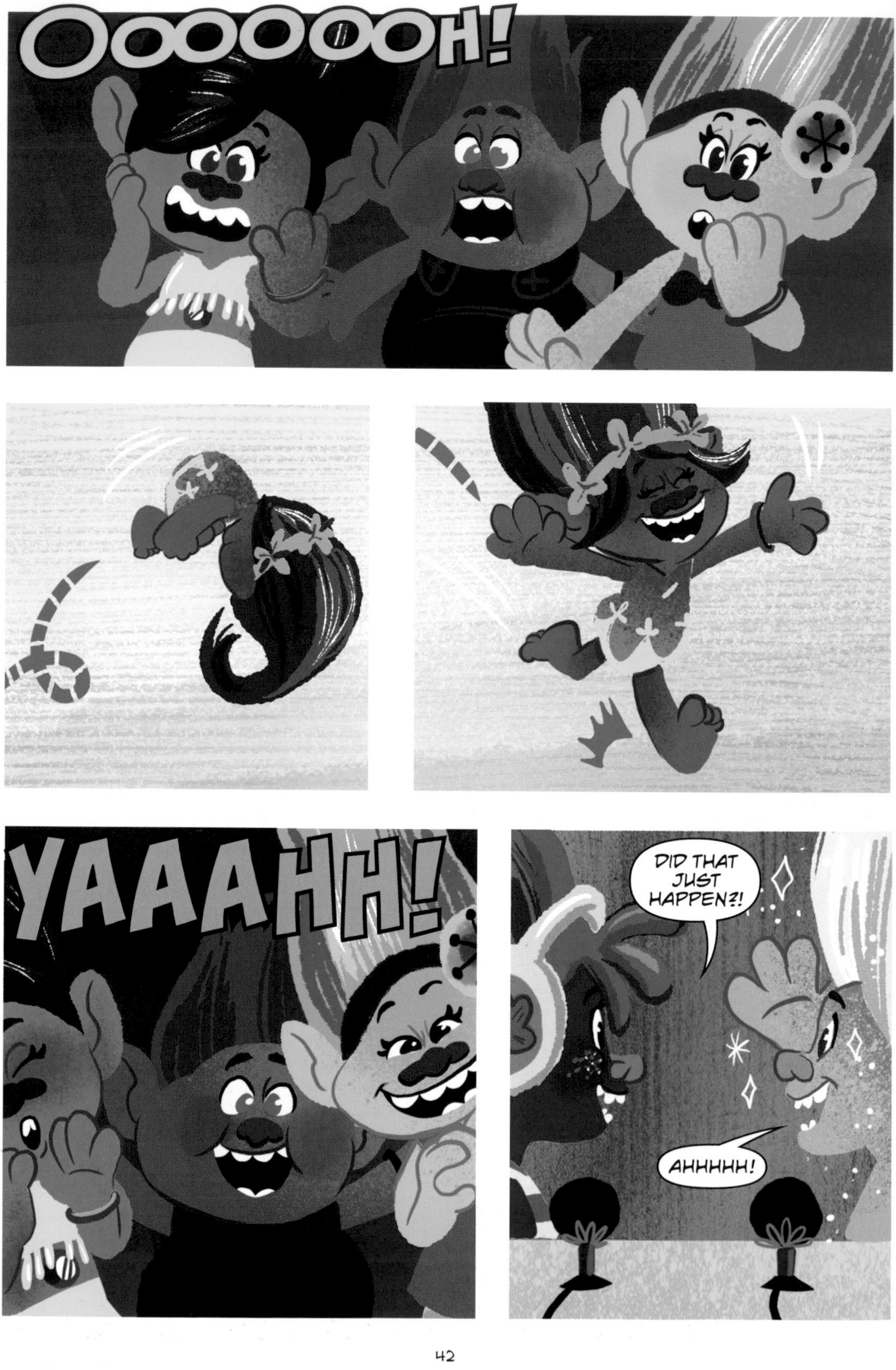
OOOOOOH!
YAAAHH!
DID THAT JUST HAPPEN?!
AHHHHH!

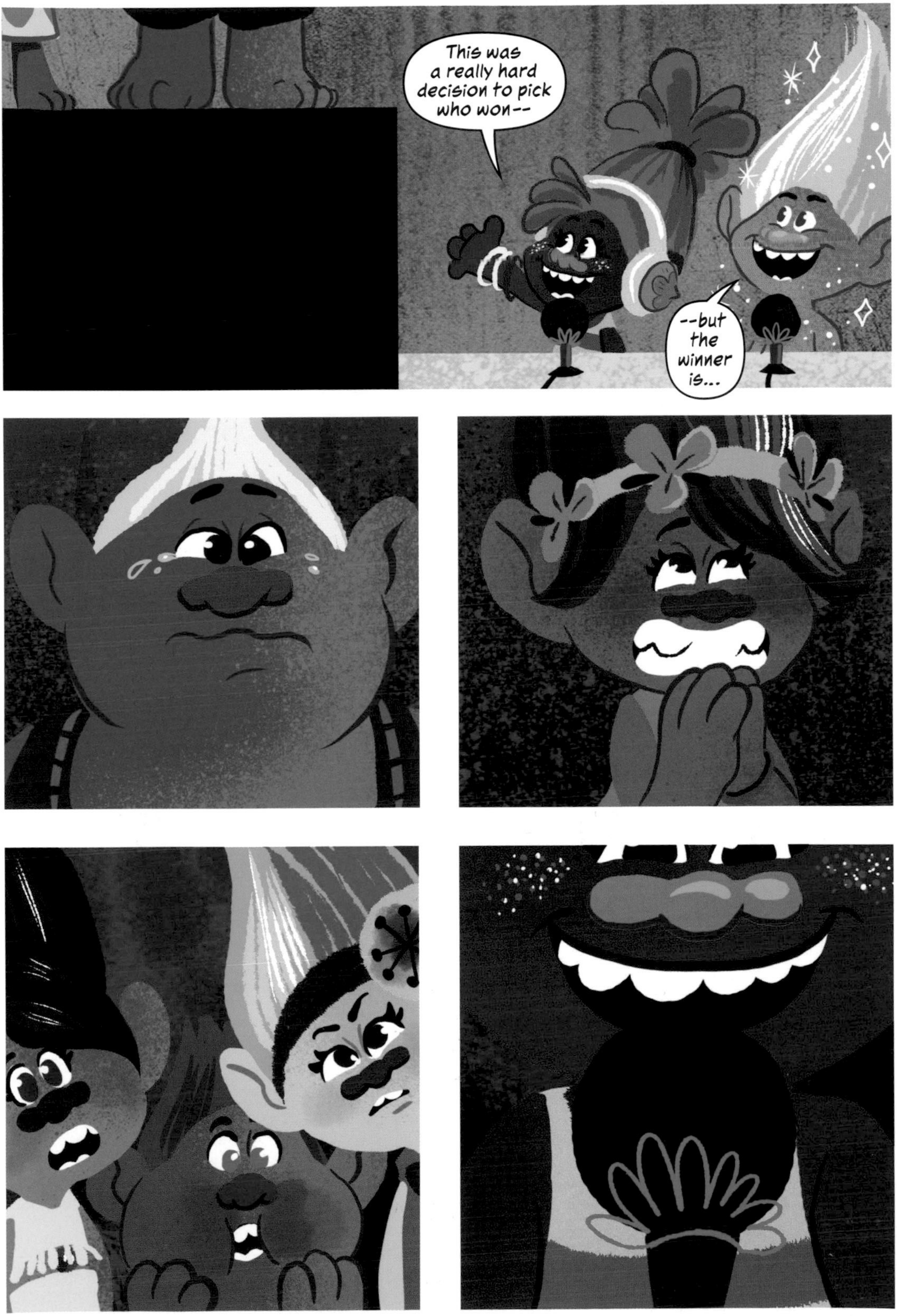
[redacted]
This was a really hard decision to pick who won--
--but the winner is...

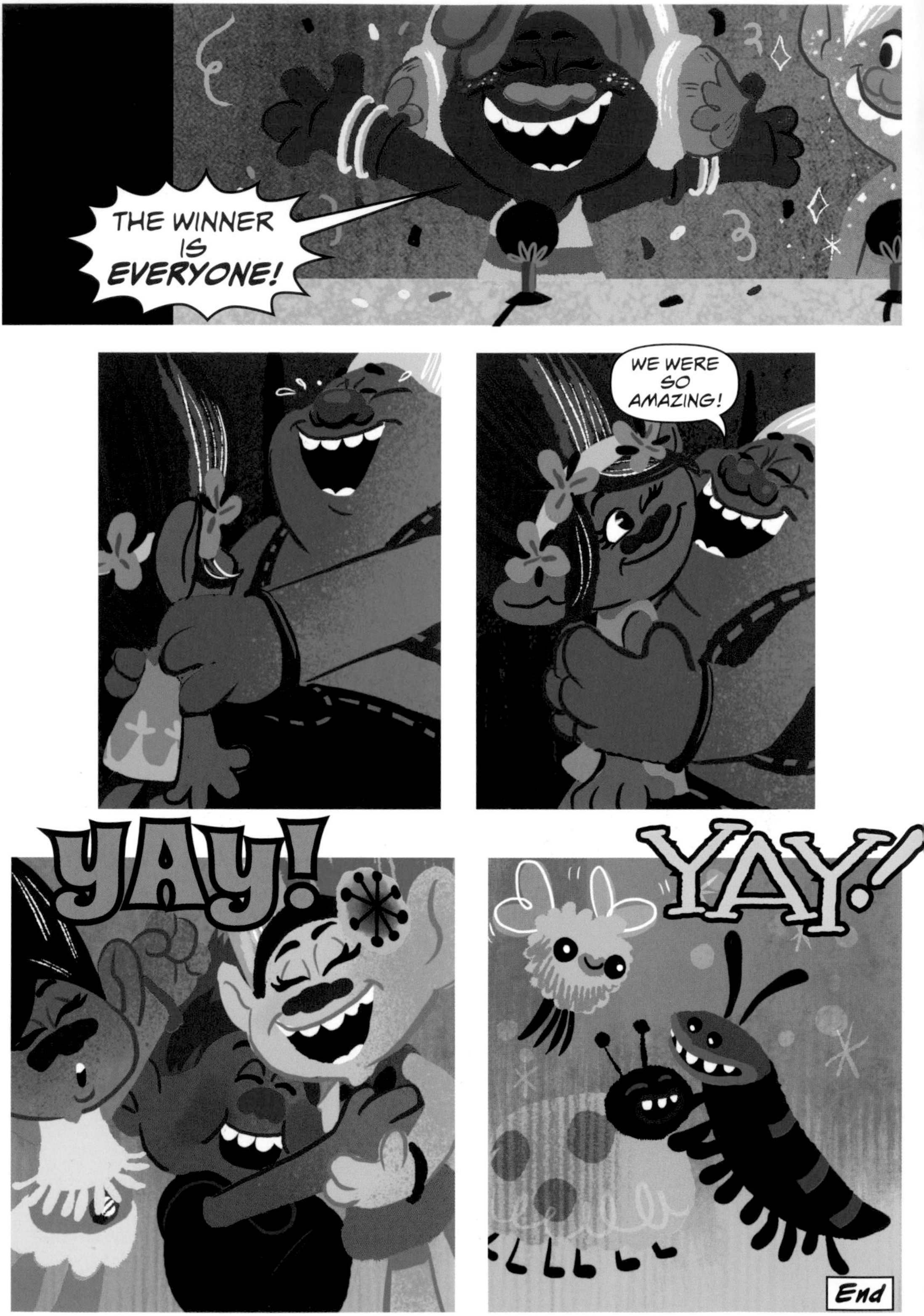
THE WINNER IS EVERYONE!
WE WERE SO AMAZING!
YAY!
YAY!
End

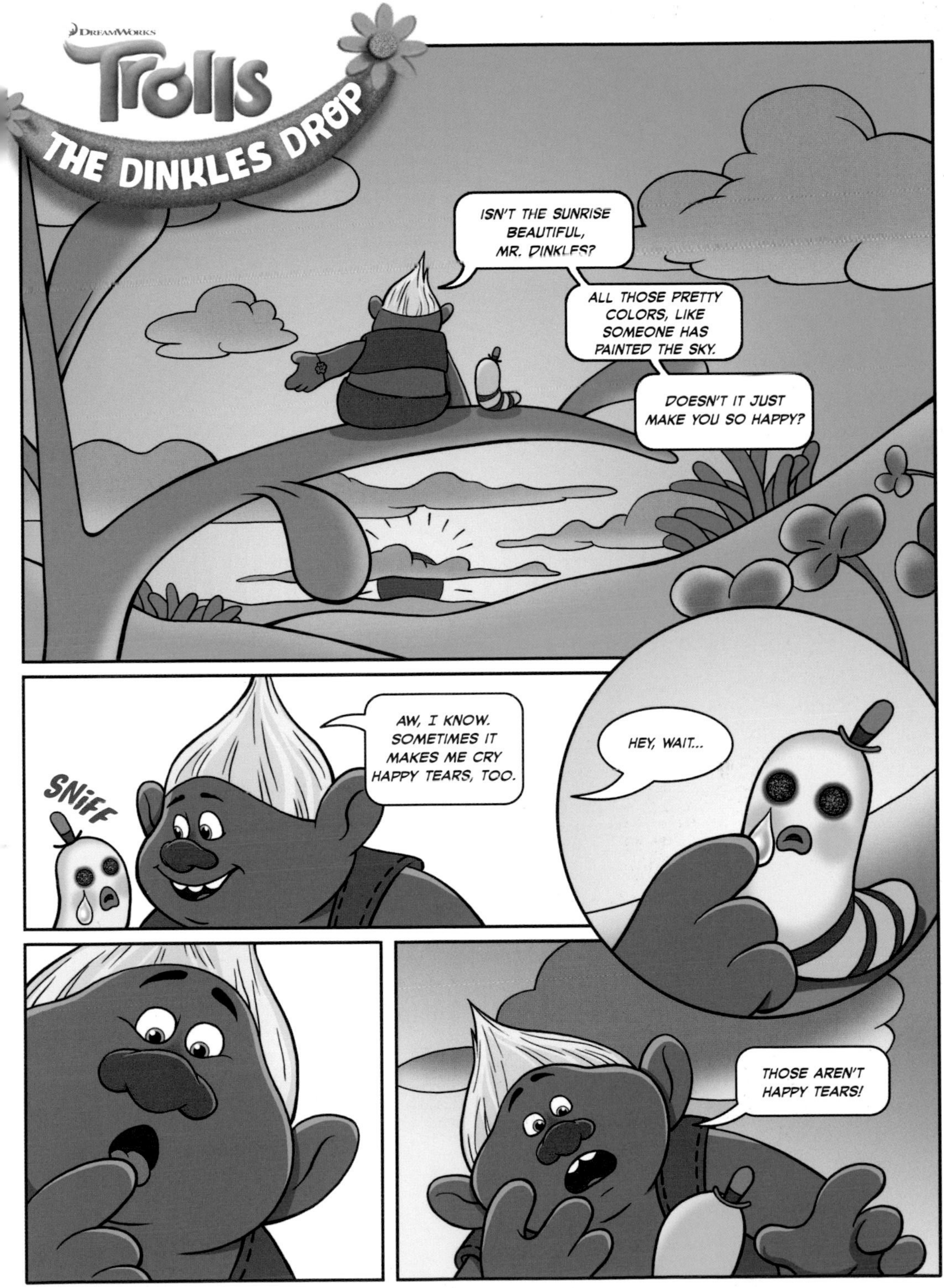
DreamWorks
Trolls
THE DINKLES DROP
ISN'T THE SUNRISE BEAUTIFUL, MR. DINKLES?
ALL THOSE PRETTY COLORS, LIKE SOMEONE HAS PAINTED THE SKY.
DOESN'T IT JUST MAKE YOU SO HAPPY?
SNIFF
AW, I KNOW. SOMETIMES IT MAKES ME CRY HAPPY TEARS, TOO.
HEY, WAIT...
THOSE AREN'T HAPPY TEARS!

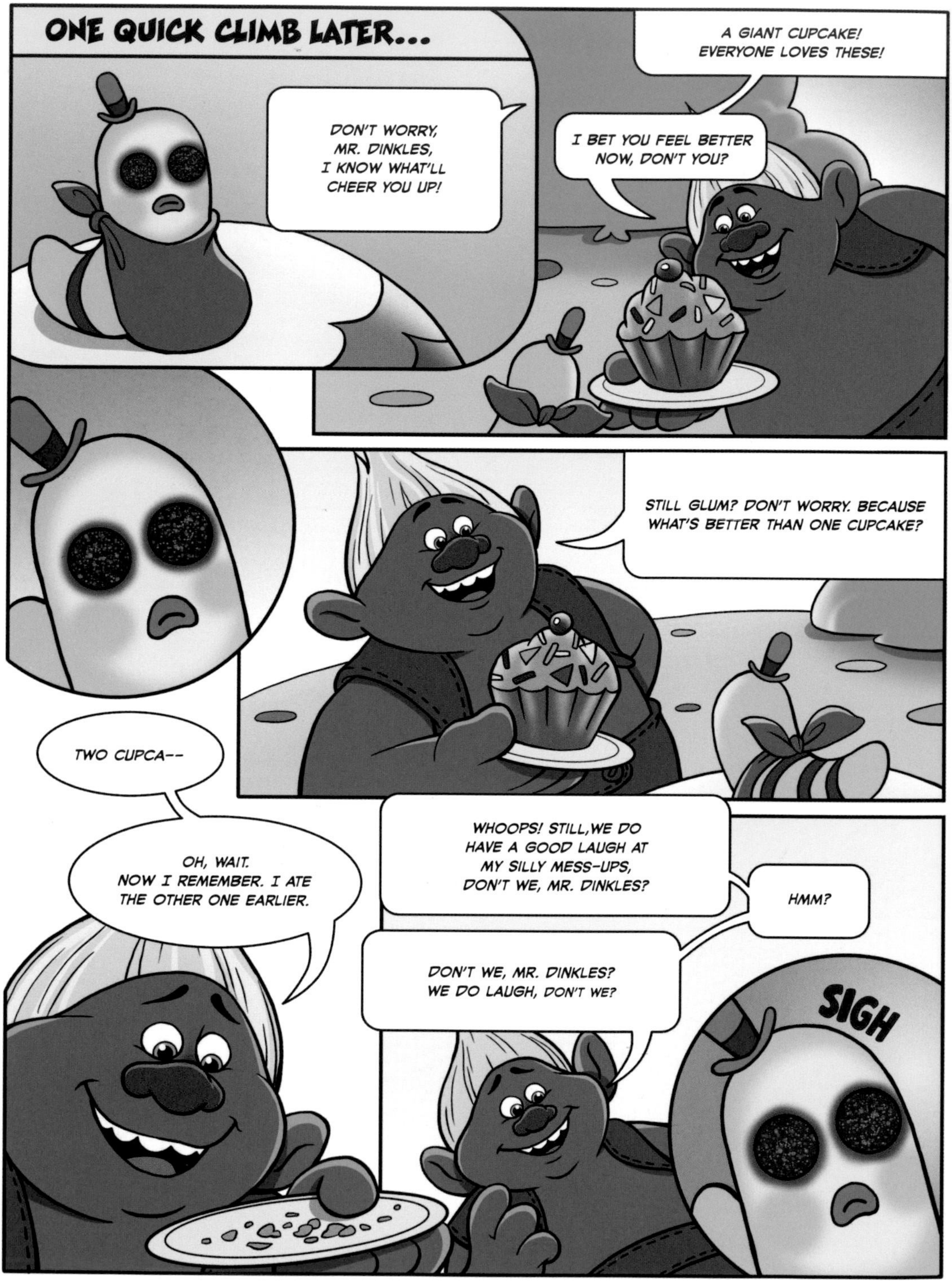
ONE QUICK CLIMB LATER...
DON'T WORRY, MR. DINKLES, I KNOW WHAT'LL CHEER YOU UP!
A GIANT CUPCAKE! EVERYONE LOVES THESE!
I BET YOU FEEL BETTER NOW, DON'T YOU?
STILL GLUM? DON'T WORRY. BECAUSE WHAT'S BETTER THAN ONE CUPCAKE?
TWO CUPCA--
OH, WAIT. NOW I REMEMBER. I ATE THE OTHER ONE EARLIER.
WHOOPS! STILL,WE DO HAVE A GOOD LAUGH AT MY SILLY MESS-UPS, DON'T WE, MR. DINKLES?
HMM?
DON'T WE, MR. DINKLES? WE DO LAUGH, DON'T WE?
SIGH

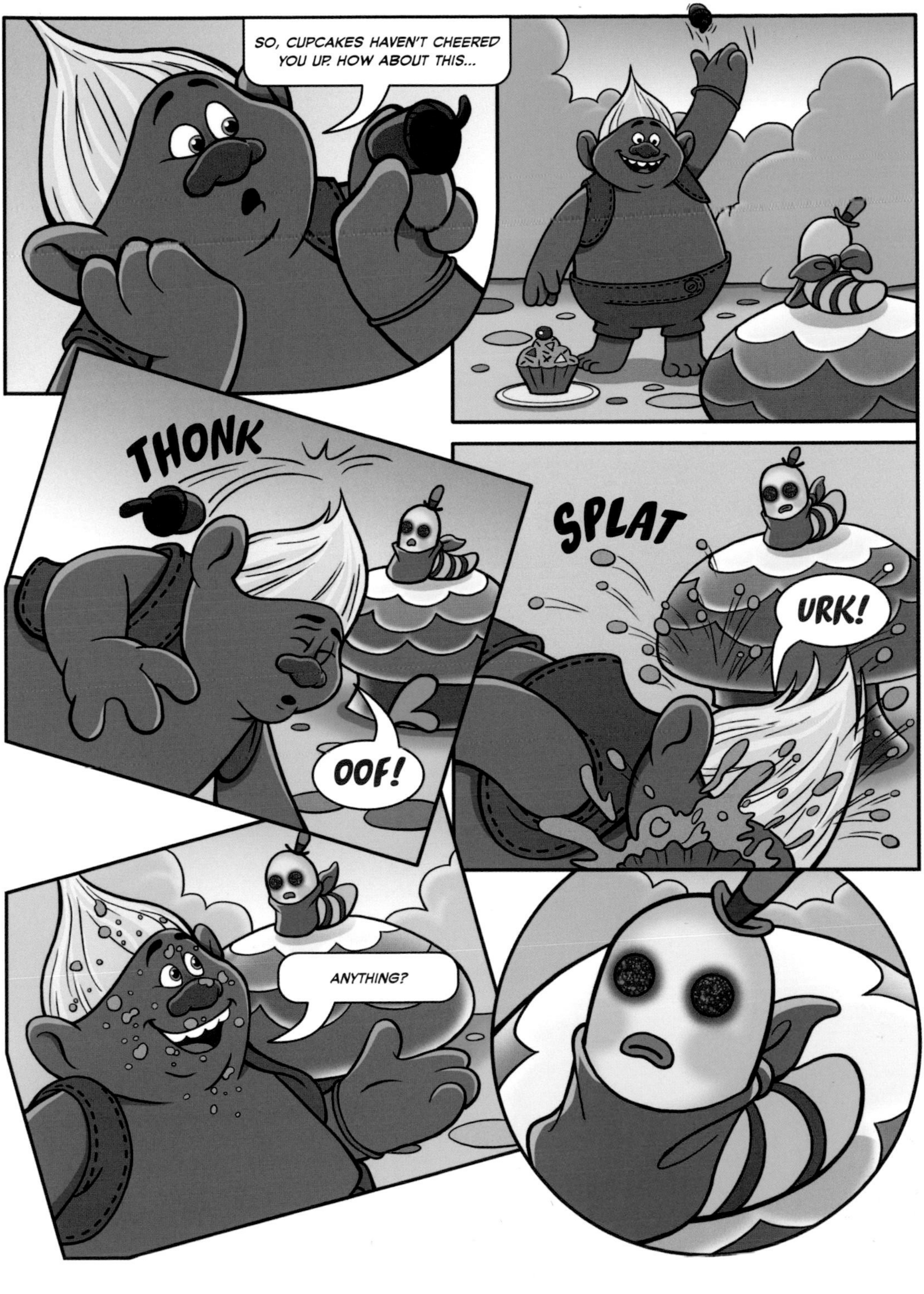
SO, CUPCAKES HAVEN'T CHEERED YOU UP. HOW ABOUT THIS...
THONK
OOF!
SPLAT
URK!
ANYTHING?

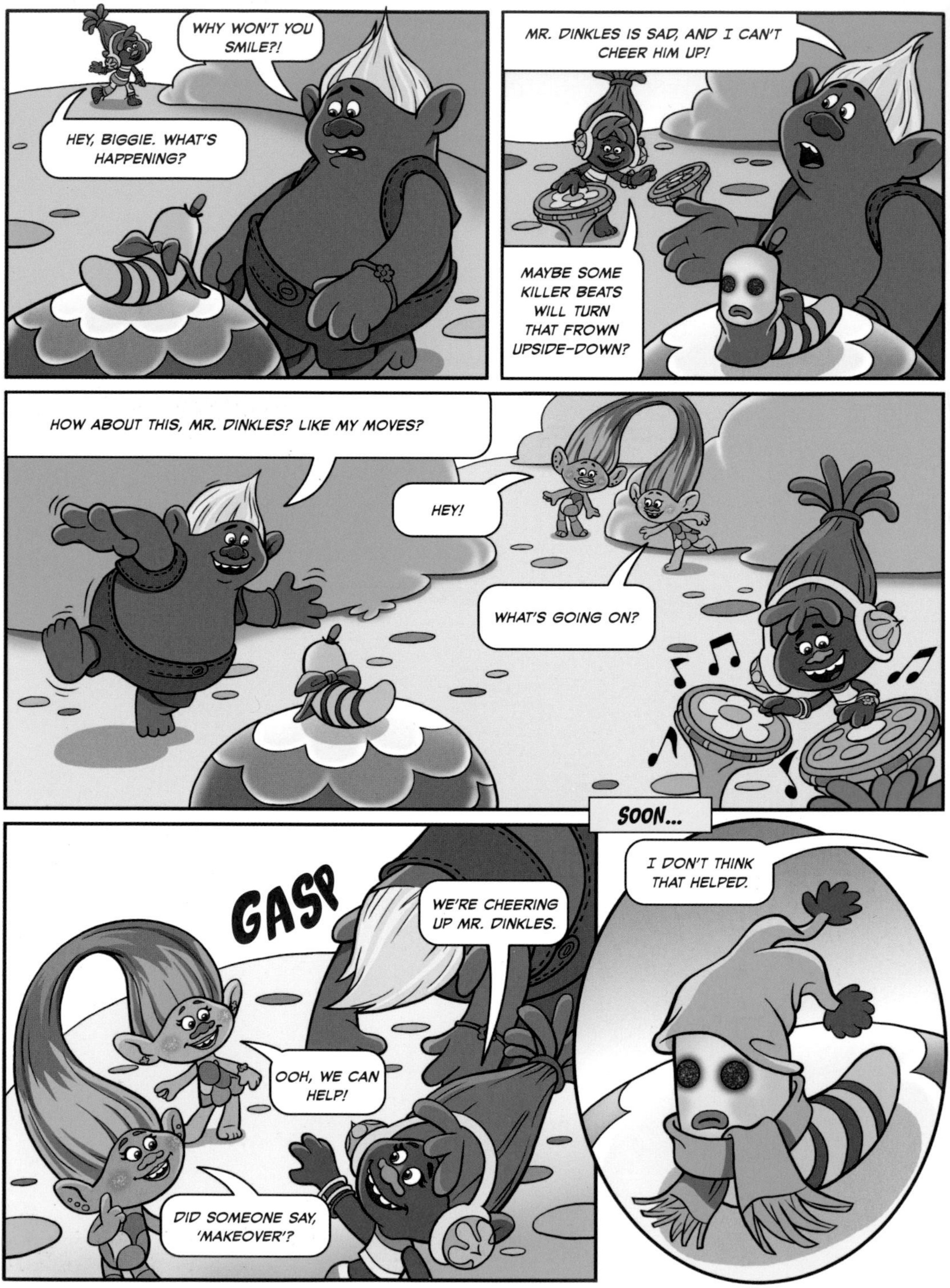
HEY, BIGGIE. WHAT'S HAPPENING?
WHY WON'T YOU SMILE?!
MR. DINKLES IS SAD, AND I CAN'T CHEER HIM UP!
MAYBE SOME KILLER BEATS WILL TURN THAT FROWN UPSIDE-DOWN?
HOW ABOUT THIS, MR. DINKLES? LIKE MY MOVES?
HEY!
WHAT'S GOING ON?
SOON...
GASP
WE'RE CHEERING UP MR. DINKLES.
OOH, WE CAN HELP!
DID SOMEONE SAY, 'MAKEOVER'?
I DON'T THINK THAT HELPED.

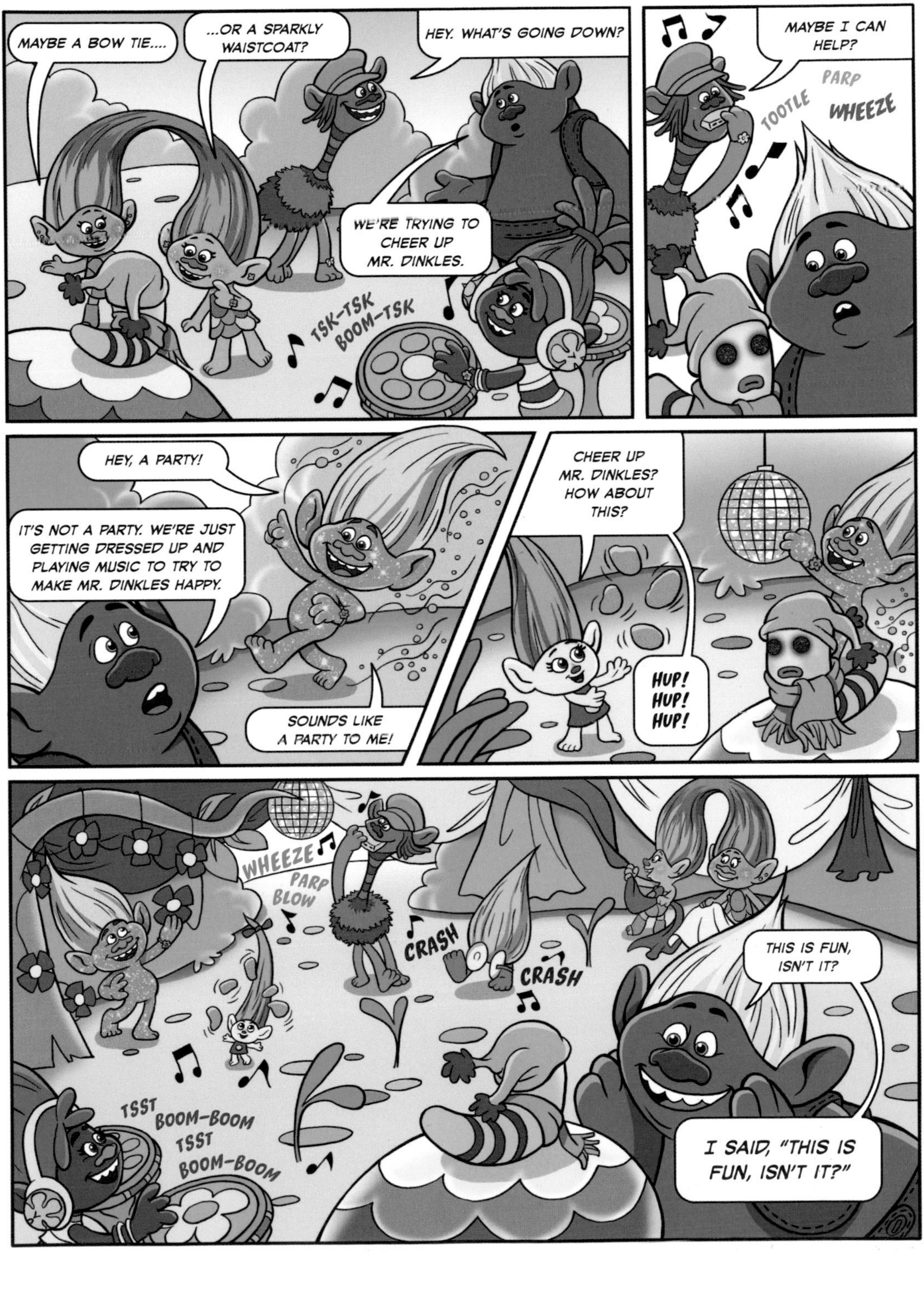
MAYBE A BOW TIE....
...OR A SPARKLY WAISTCOAT?
HEY. WHAT'S GOING DOWN?
WE'RE TRYING TO CHEER UP MR. DINKLES.
TSK-TSK BOOM-TSK
MAYBE I CAN HELP?
PARP
TOOTLE
WHEEZE
HEY, A PARTY!
IT'S NOT A PARTY. WE'RE JUST GETTING DRESSED UP AND PLAYING MUSIC TO TRY TO MAKE MR. DINKLES HAPPY.
SOUNDS LIKE A PARTY TO ME!
CHEER UP MR. DINKLES? HOW ABOUT THIS?
HUP! HUP! HUP!
WHEEZE
PARP
BLOW
CRASH
CRASH
THIS IS FUN, ISN'T IT?
TSST
BOOM-BOOM
TSST
BOOM-BOOM
I SAID, "THIS IS FUN, ISN'T IT?"

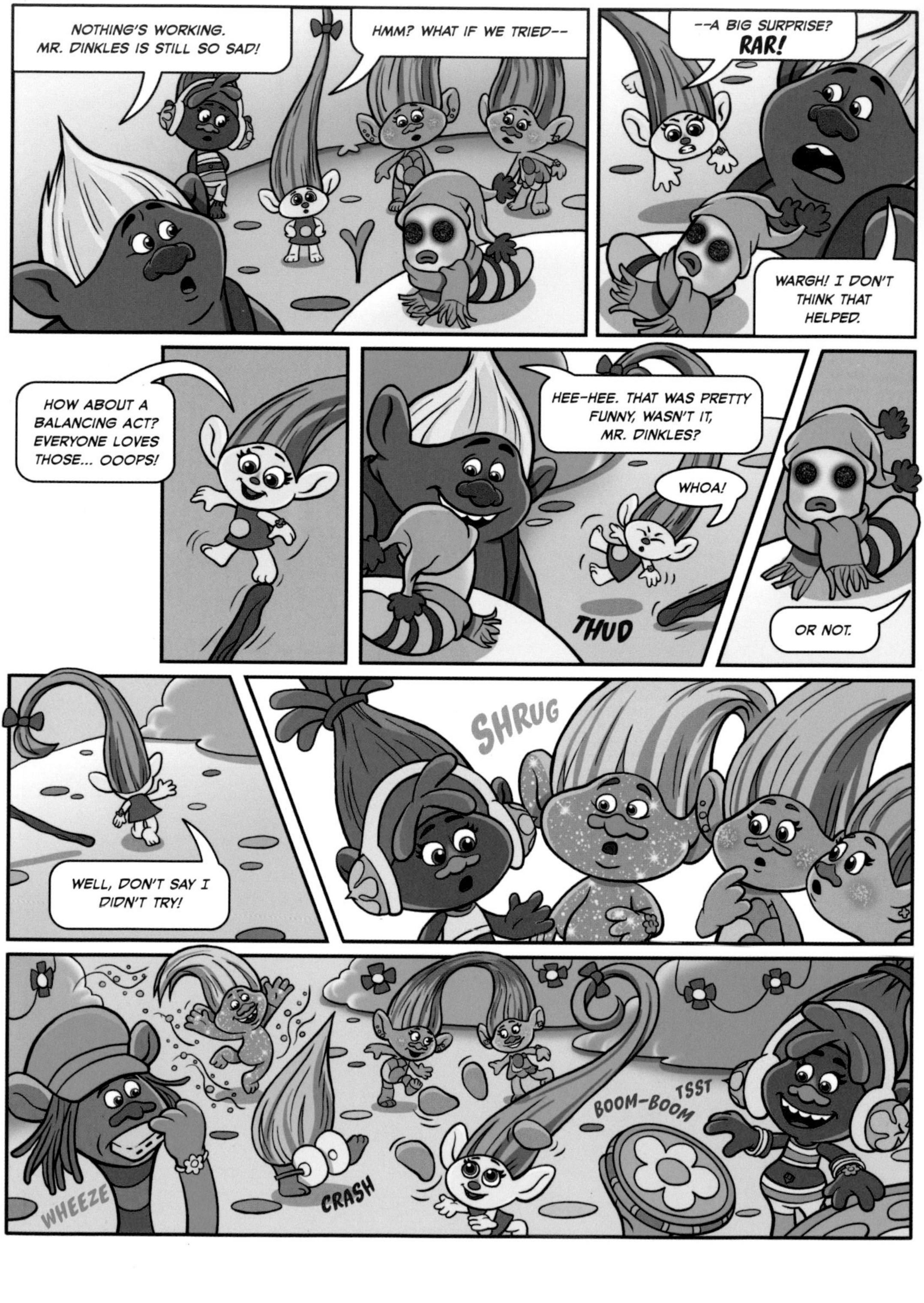
NOTHING'S WORKING. MR. DINKLES IS STILL SO SAD!
HMM? WHAT IF WE TRIED--
--A BIG SURPRISE? RAR!
WARGH! I DON'T THINK THAT HELPED.
HOW ABOUT A BALANCING ACT? EVERYONE LOVES THOSE... OOOPS!
HEE-HEE. THAT WAS PRETTY FUNNY, WASN'T IT, MR. DINKLES?
WHOA!
THUD
OR NOT.
WELL, DON'T SAY I DIDN'T TRY!
SHRUG
TSST
BOOM-BOOM
WHEEZE
CRASH

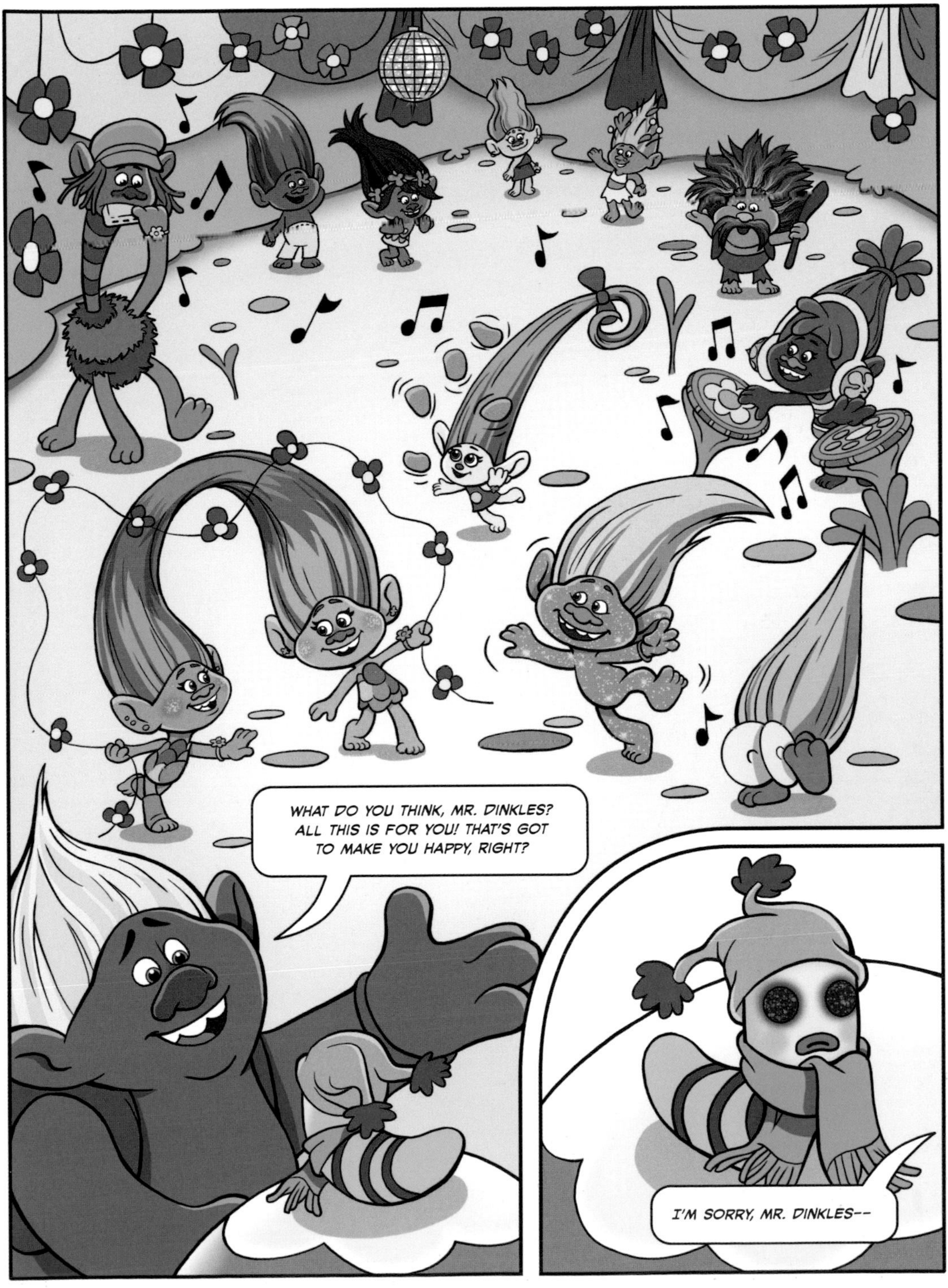
WHAT DO YOU THINK, MR. DINKLES? ALL THIS IS FOR YOU! THAT'S GOT TO MAKE YOU HAPPY, RIGHT?
I'M SORRY, MR. DINKLES--

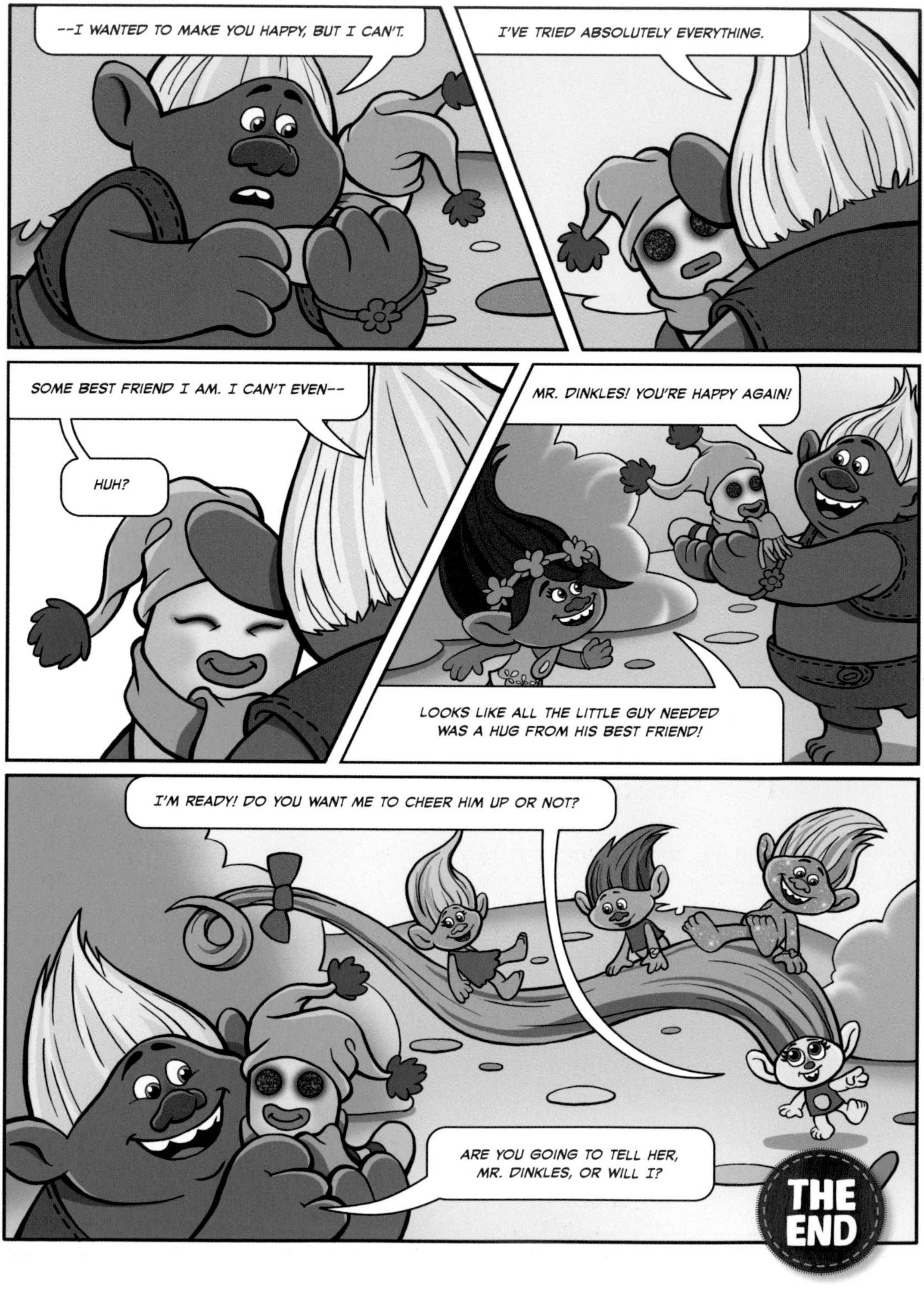
--I WANTED TO MAKE YOU HAPPY, BUT I CAN'T.
I'VE TRIED ABSOLUTELY EVERYTHING.
SOME BEST FRIEND I AM. I CAN'T EVEN--
HUH?
MR. DINKLES! YOU'RE HAPPY AGAIN!
LOOKS LIKE ALL THE LITTLE GUY NEEDED WAS A HUG FROM HIS BEST FRIEND!
I'M READY! DO YOU WANT ME TO CHEER HIM UP OR NOT?
ARE YOU GOING TO TELL HER, MR. DINKLES, OR WILL I?
THE END

Class Visitors

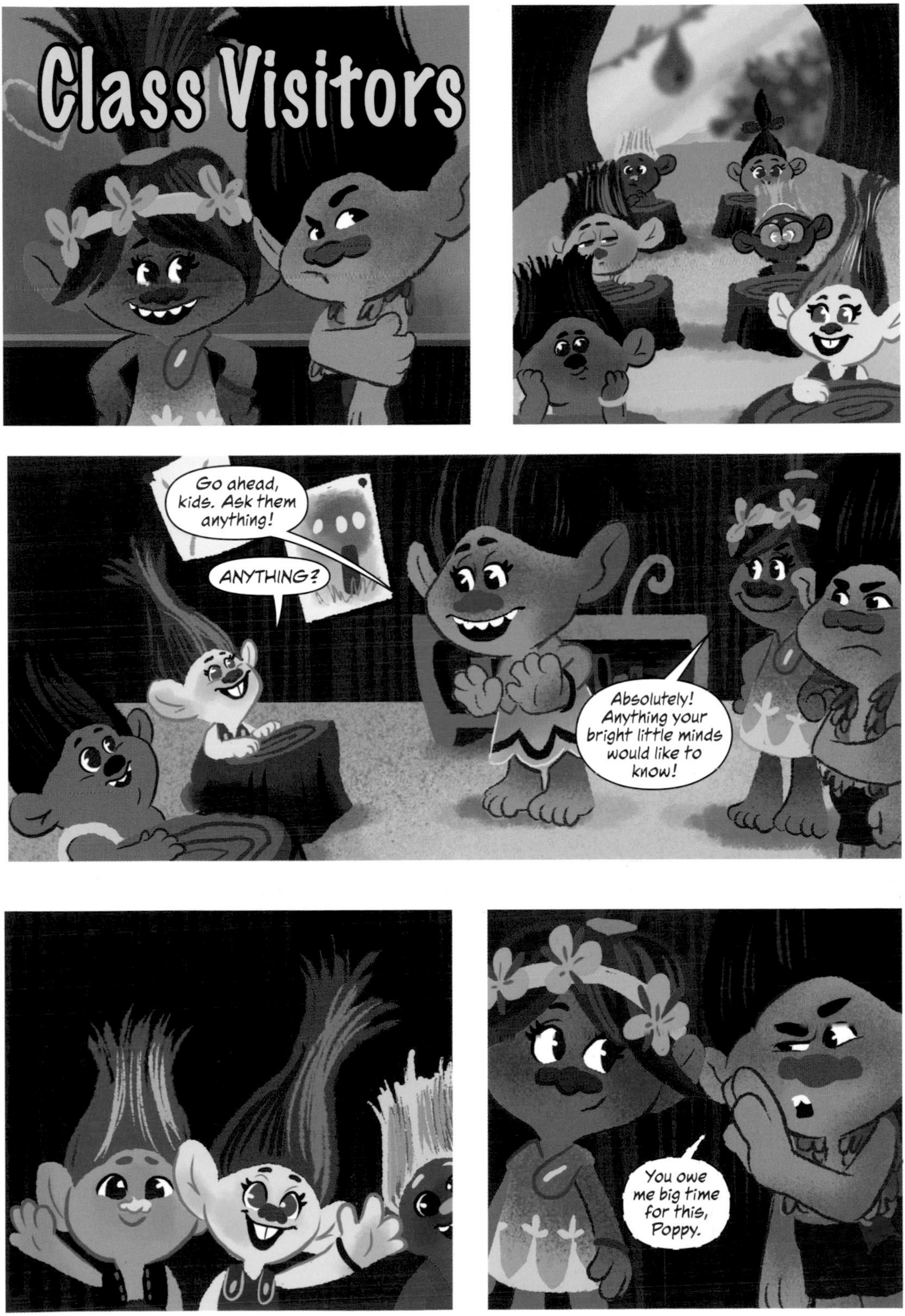

Go ahead, kids. Ask them anything!
ANYTHING?
Absolutely! Anything your bright little minds would like to know!
You owe me big time for this, Poppy.

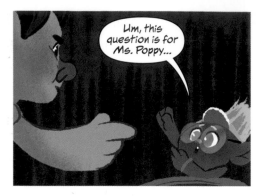

Um, this question is for Ms. Poppy...

What's your favorite part about being a Troll?

I love my family!

I love my friends!

I love my hair!

I love absolutely everything about being a Troll!

Any questions for Branch?

What's your favorite part about Poppy?

Her beautiful smile.

Next question.

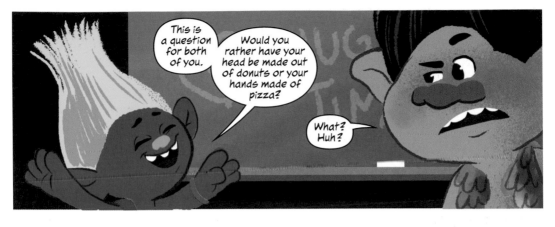

This is a question for both of you.

Would you rather have your head be made out of donuts or your hands made of pizza?

What? Huh?

I would rather have a donut for a head because then everyone would know how sweet I am!

This question is for Branch!

What's your question?

Can I go to the bathroom?

Um, sure.

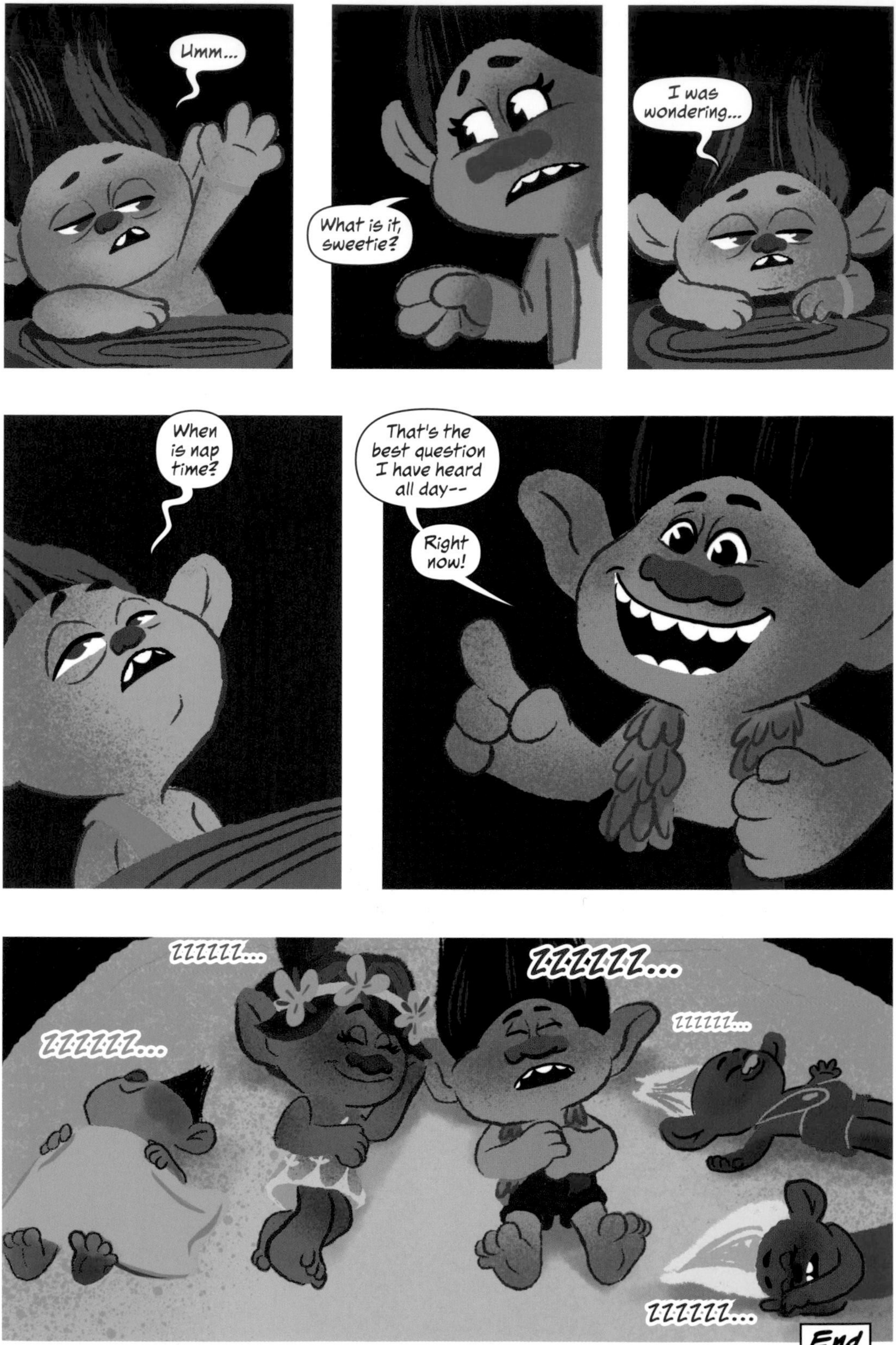
Umm...
What is it, sweetie?
I was wondering...
When is nap time?
That's the best question I have heard all day--
Right now!
ZZZZZZ...
ZZZZZZ...
ZZZZZZ...
ZZZZZZ...
ZZZZZZ...
End

Special Preview of THE SISTERS #2 "Doing It Our Way!"

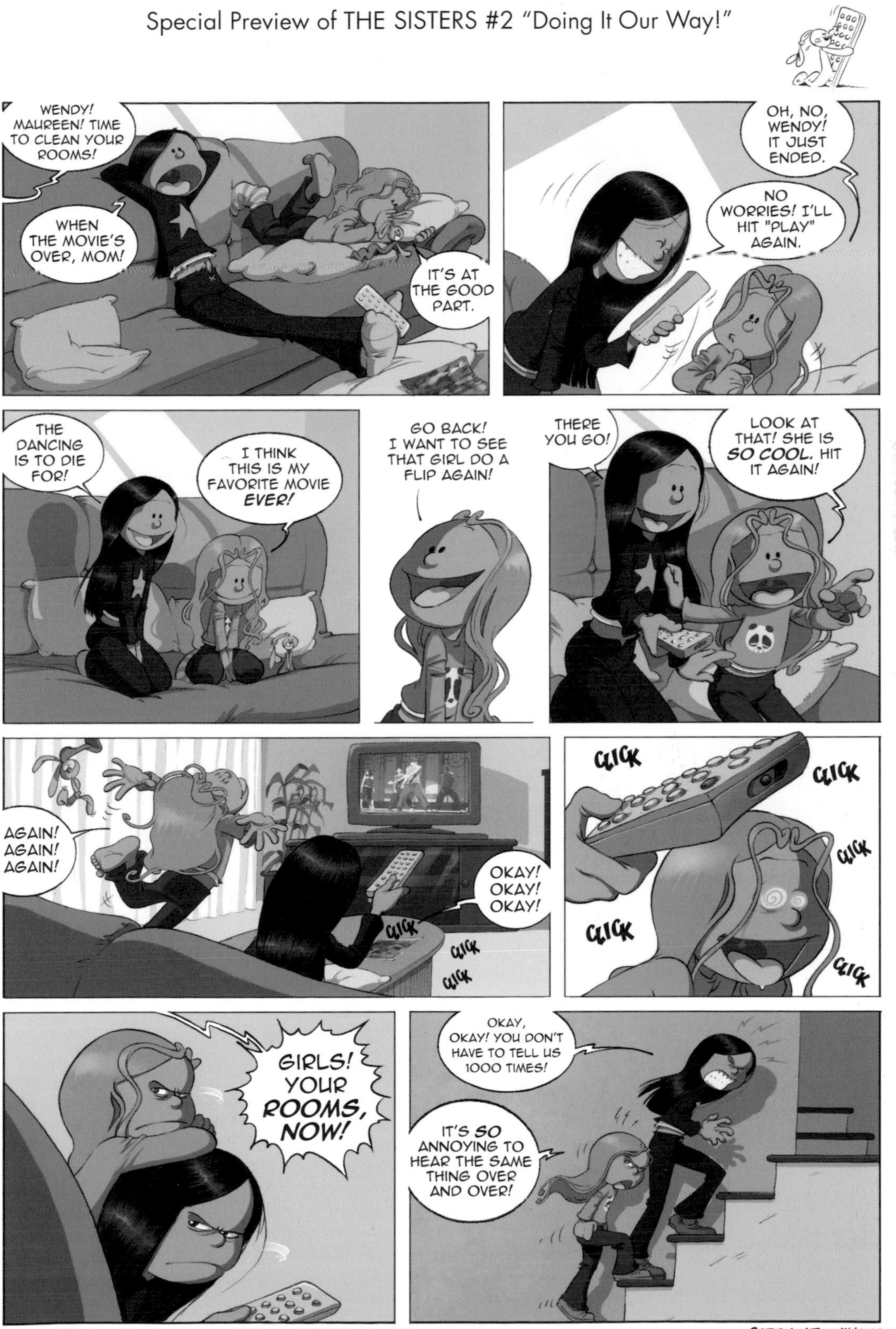

WENDY! MAUREEN! TIME TO CLEAN YOUR ROOMS!
WHEN THE MOVIE'S OVER, MOM!
IT'S AT THE GOOD PART.
OH, NO, WENDY! IT JUST ENDED.
NO WORRIES! I'LL HIT "PLAY" AGAIN.
THE DANCING IS TO DIE FOR!
I THINK THIS IS MY FAVORITE MOVIE EVER!
GO BACK! I WANT TO SEE THAT GIRL DO A FLIP AGAIN!
THERE YOU GO!
LOOK AT THAT! SHE IS SO COOL. HIT IT AGAIN!
AGAIN! AGAIN! AGAIN!
OKAY! OKAY! OKAY!
CLICK
CLICK
CLICK
CLICK
CLICK
CLICK
CLICK
CLICK
GIRLS! YOUR ROOMS, NOW!
OKAY, OKAY! YOU DON'T HAVE TO TELL US 1000 TIMES!
IT'S SO ANNOYING TO HEAR THE SAME THING OVER AND OVER!
CAZENOVE & WILLIAM

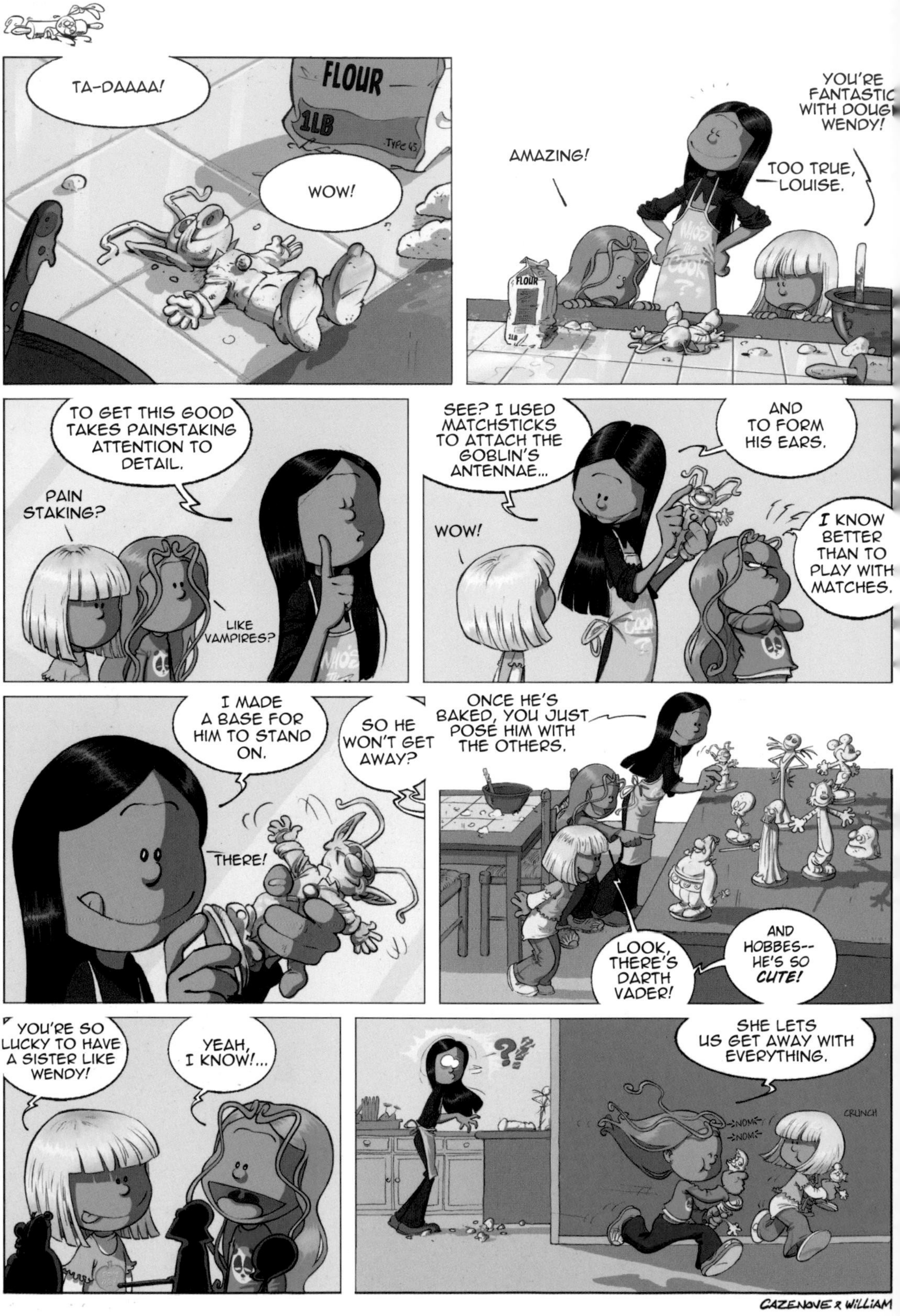
TA-DAAAA!
FLOUR
1LB
WOW!
AMAZING!
YOU'RE FANTASTIC WITH DOUGH WENDY!
TOO TRUE, LOUISE.
TO GET THIS GOOD TAKES PAINSTAKING ATTENTION TO DETAIL.
PAIN STAKING?
LIKE VAMPIRES?
SEE? I USED MATCHSTICKS TO ATTACH THE GOBLIN'S ANTENNAE...
AND TO FORM HIS EARS.
WOW!
I KNOW BETTER THAN TO PLAY WITH MATCHES.
I MADE A BASE FOR HIM TO STAND ON.
SO HE WON'T GET AWAY?
THERE!
ONCE HE'S BAKED, YOU JUST POSE HIM WITH THE OTHERS.
LOOK, THERE'S DARTH VADER!
AND HOBBES-- HE'S SO CUTE!
YOU'RE SO LUCKY TO HAVE A SISTER LIKE WENDY!
YEAH, I KNOW!...
SHE LETS US GET AWAY WITH EVERYTHING.
NOM NOM
CRUNCH
CAZENOVE & WILLIAM

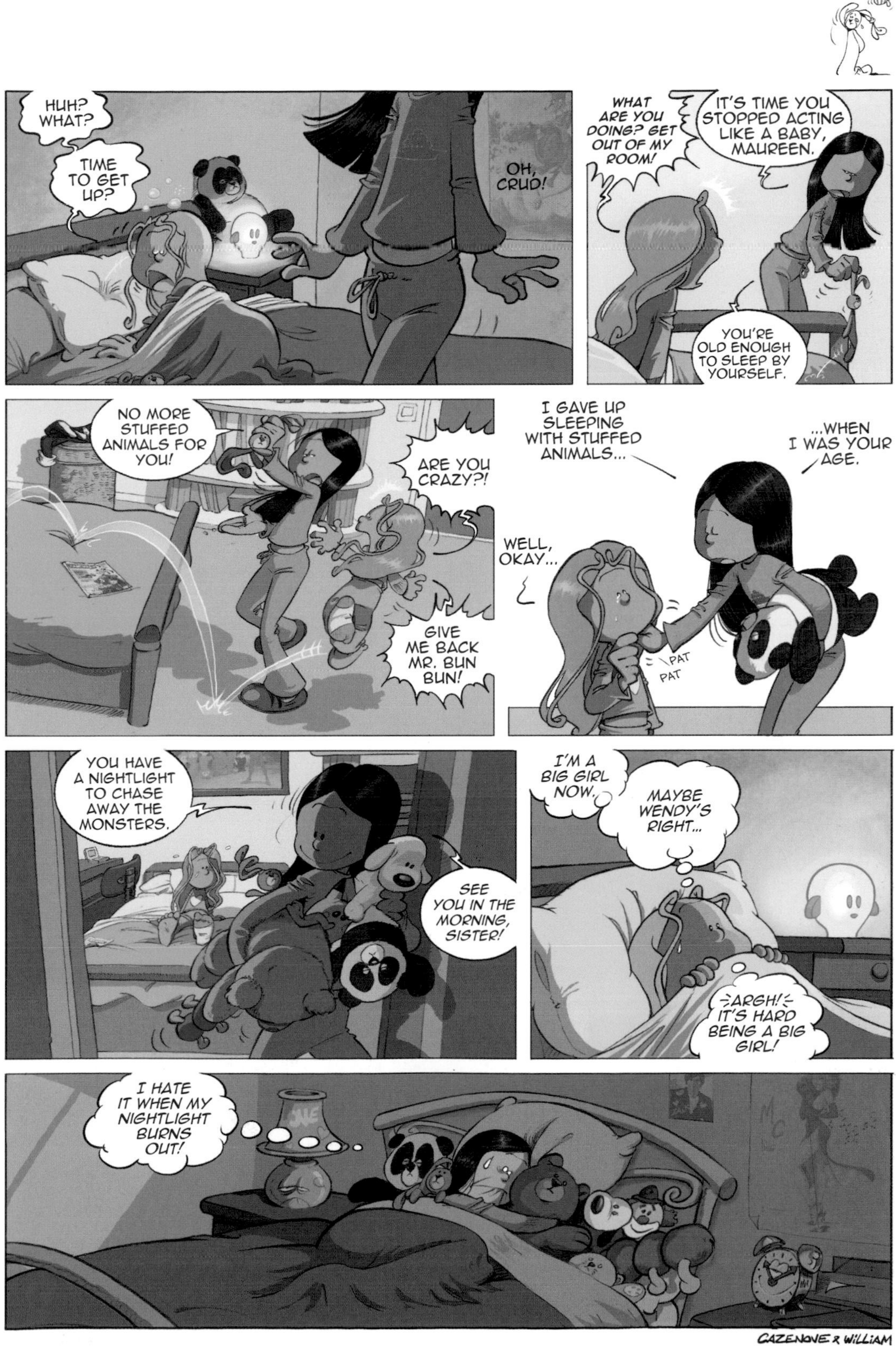
HUH? WHAT?
TIME TO GET UP?
OH, CRUD!
WHAT ARE YOU DOING? GET OUT OF MY ROOM!
IT'S TIME YOU STOPPED ACTING LIKE A BABY, MAUREEN.
YOU'RE OLD ENOUGH TO SLEEP BY YOURSELF.
NO MORE STUFFED ANIMALS FOR YOU!
ARE YOU CRAZY?!
GIVE ME BACK MR. BUN BUN!
I GAVE UP SLEEPING WITH STUFFED ANIMALS...
...WHEN I WAS YOUR AGE.
WELL, OKAY...
PAT
PAT
YOU HAVE A NIGHTLIGHT TO CHASE AWAY THE MONSTERS.
SEE YOU IN THE MORNING, SISTER!
I'M A BIG GIRL NOW.
MAYBE WENDY'S RIGHT...
ARGH! IT'S HARD BEING A BIG GIRL!
I HATE IT WHEN MY NIGHTLIGHT BURNS OUT!
CAZENOVE & WILLIAM

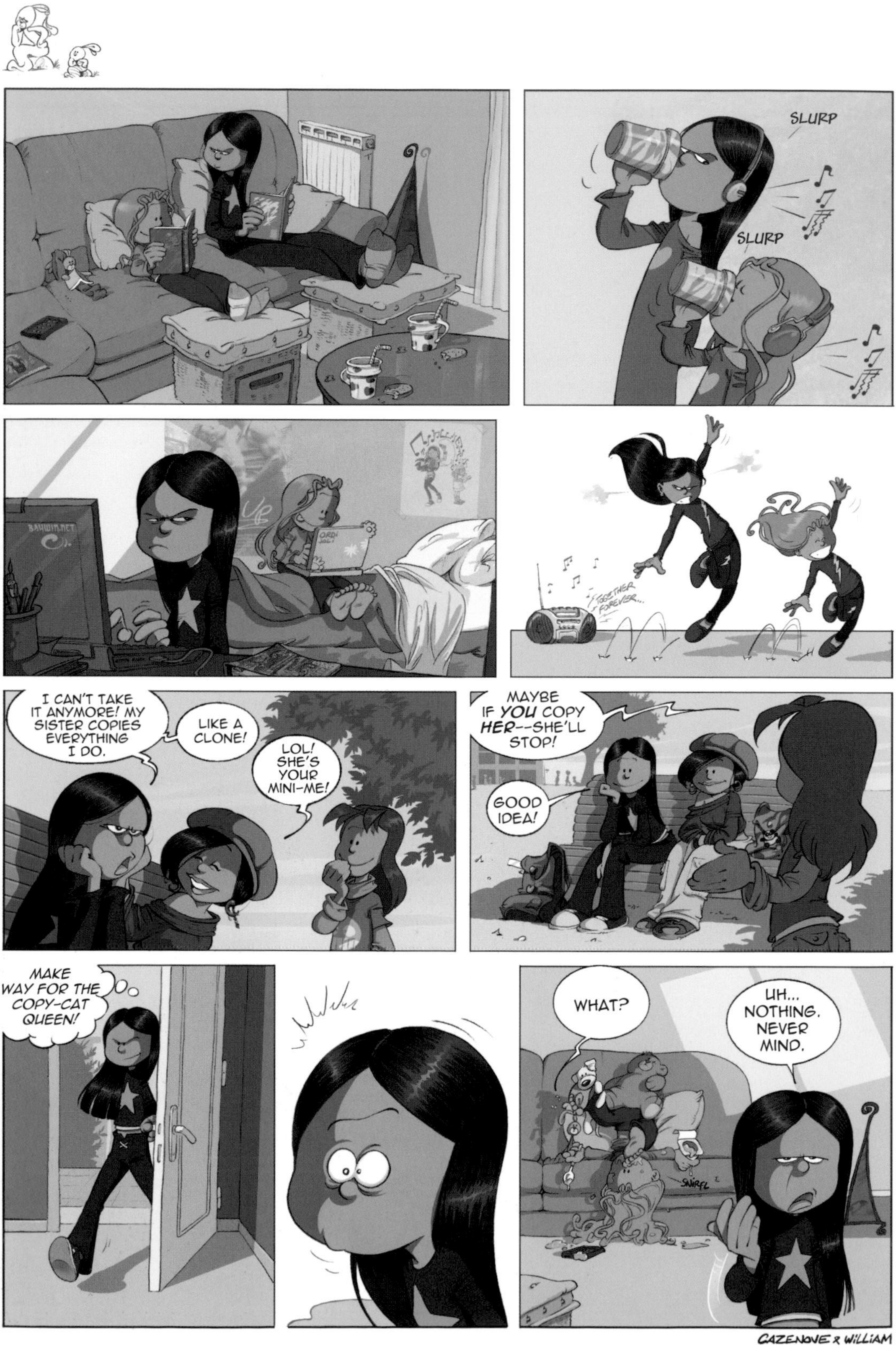
SLURP
SLURP
TOGETHER FOREVER...
I CAN'T TAKE IT ANYMORE! MY SISTER COPIES EVERYTHING I DO.
LIKE A CLONE!
LOL! SHE'S YOUR MINI-ME!
MAYBE IF YOU COPY HER--SHE'LL STOP!
GOOD IDEA!
MAKE WAY FOR THE COPY-CAT QUEEN!
WHAT?
UH... NOTHING. NEVER MIND.
SNIFFL
CAZENOVE & WILLIAM

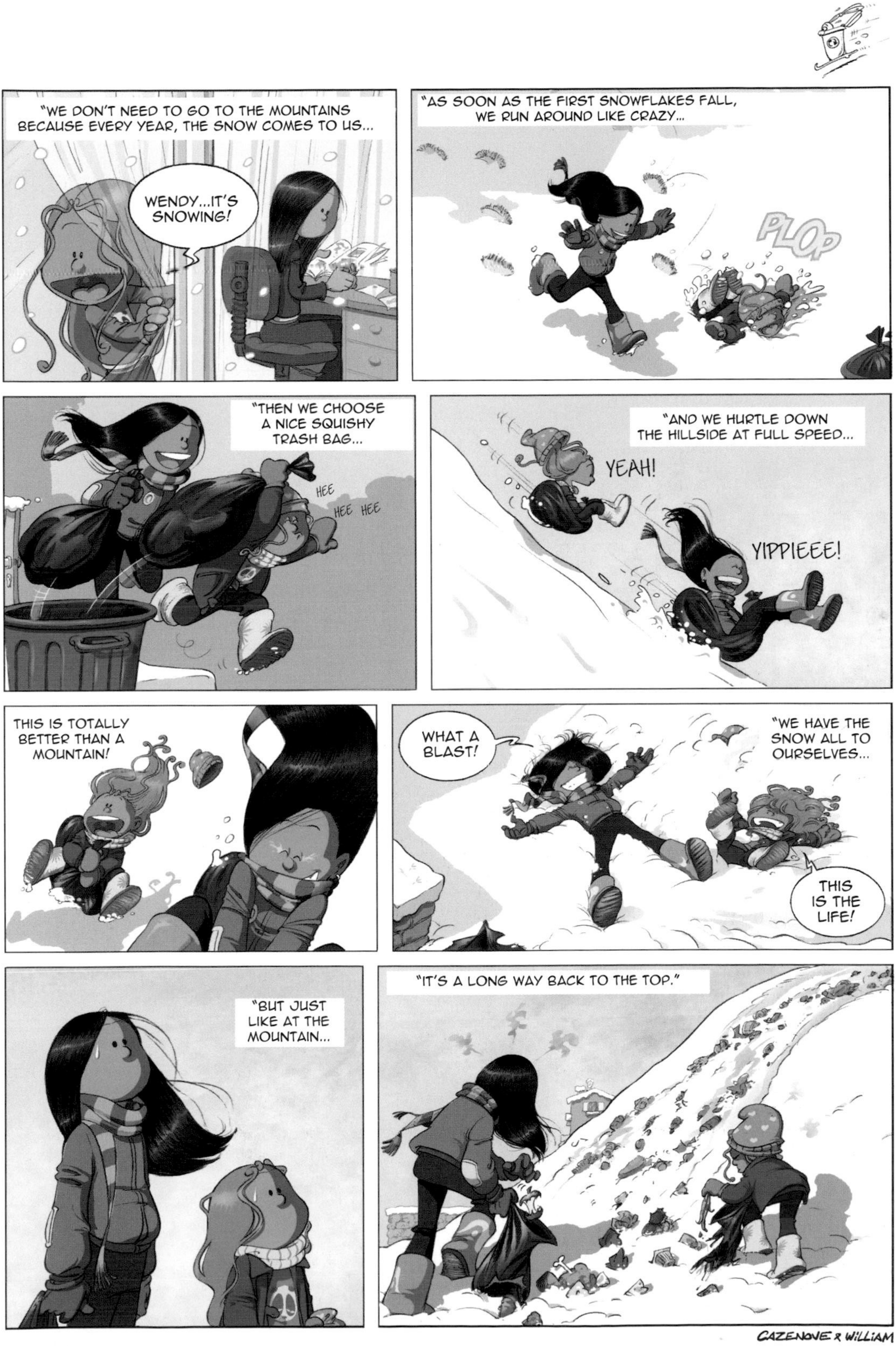

"WE DON'T NEED TO GO TO THE MOUNTAINS BECAUSE EVERY YEAR, THE SNOW COMES TO US...
WENDY...IT'S SNOWING!
"AS SOON AS THE FIRST SNOWFLAKES FALL, WE RUN AROUND LIKE CRAZY...
PLOP
"THEN WE CHOOSE A NICE SQUISHY TRASH BAG...
HEE
HEE HEE
"AND WE HURTLE DOWN THE HILLSIDE AT FULL SPEED...
YEAH!
YIPPIEEE!
THIS IS TOTALLY BETTER THAN A MOUNTAIN!
WHAT A BLAST!
"WE HAVE THE SNOW ALL TO OURSELVES...
THIS IS THE LIFE!
"BUT JUST LIKE AT THE MOUNTAIN...
"IT'S A LONG WAY BACK TO THE TOP."
CAZENOVE & WILLIAM

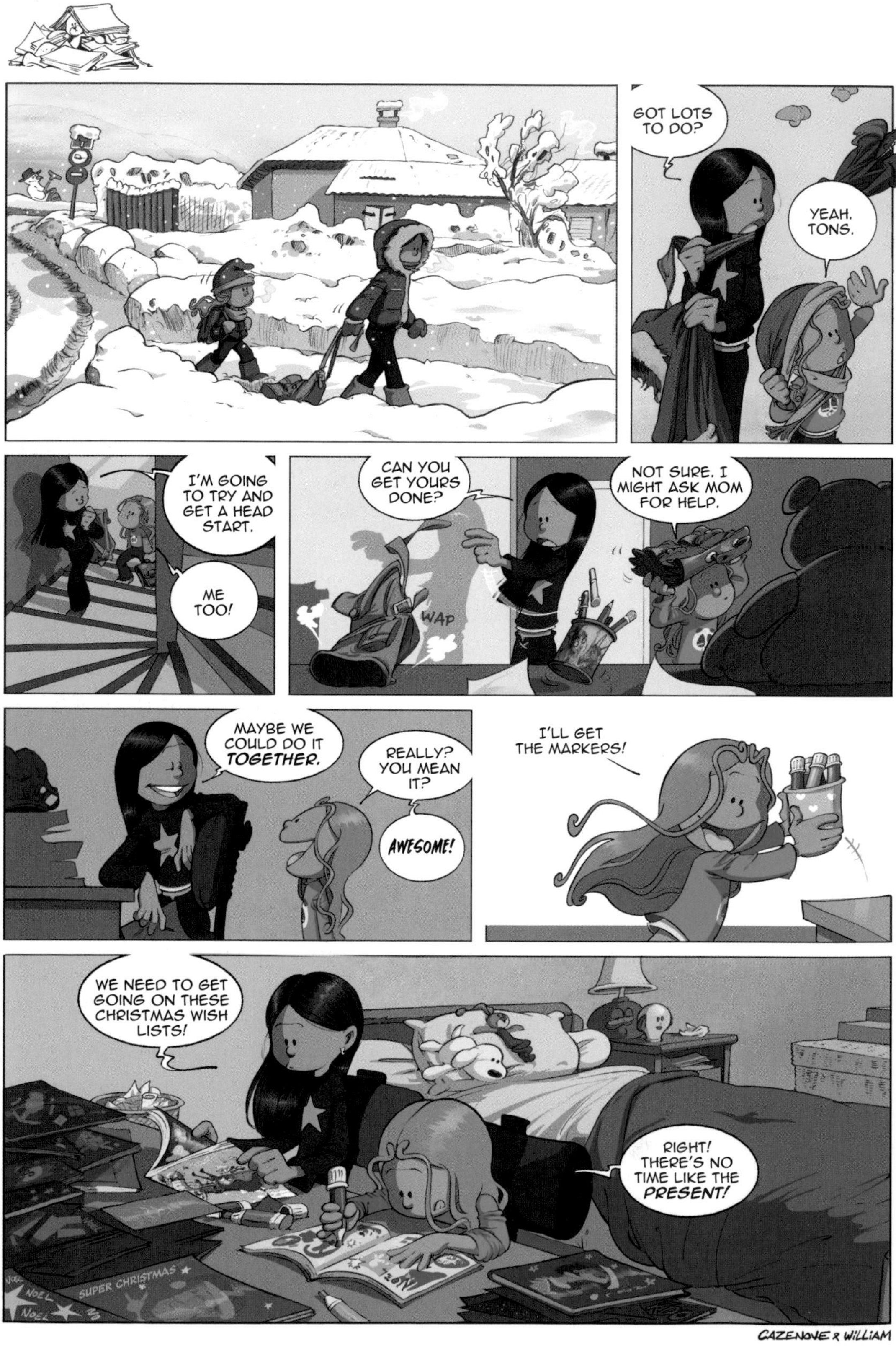

GOT LOTS TO DO?
YEAH. TONS.
I'M GOING TO TRY AND GET A HEAD START.
ME TOO!
CAN YOU GET YOURS DONE?
NOT SURE. I MIGHT ASK MOM FOR HELP.
WAP
MAYBE WE COULD DO IT *TOGETHER.*
REALLY? YOU MEAN IT?
AWESOME!
I'LL GET THE MARKERS!
WE NEED TO GET GOING ON THESE CHRISTMAS WISH LISTS!
RIGHT! THERE'S NO TIME LIKE THE *PRESENT!*
SUPER CHRISTMAS
NOEL
NOEL

CAZENOVE & WILLIAM

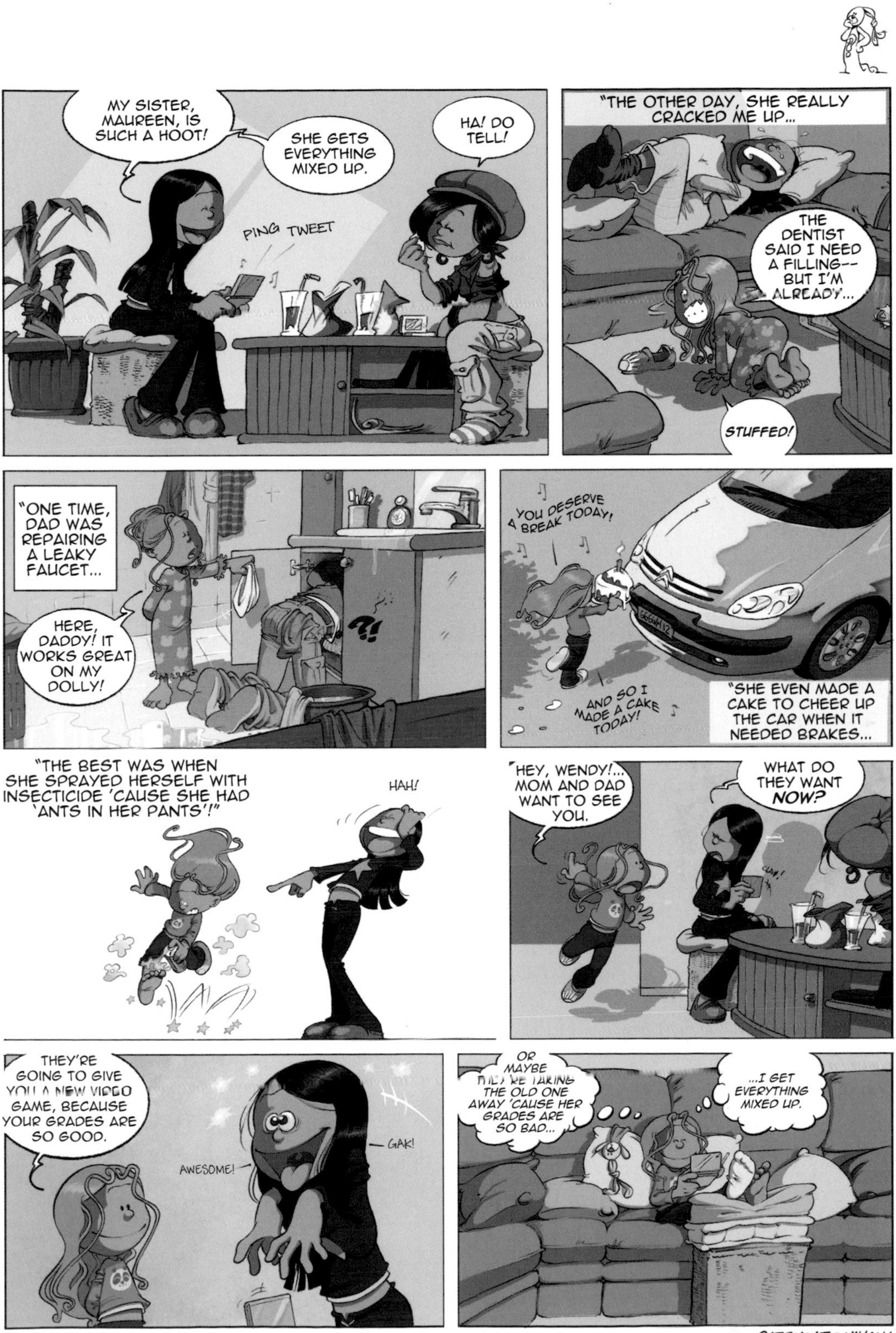
MY SISTER, MAUREEN, IS SUCH A HOOT!
SHE GETS EVERYTHING MIXED UP.
HA! DO TELL!
PING TWEET
"THE OTHER DAY, SHE REALLY CRACKED ME UP...
THE DENTIST SAID I NEED A FILLING-- BUT I'M ALREADY...
STUFFED!
"ONE TIME, DAD WAS REPAIRING A LEAKY FAUCET...
HERE, DADDY! IT WORKS GREAT ON MY DOLLY!
?!
YOU DESERVE A BREAK TODAY!
AND SO I MADE A CAKE TODAY!
"SHE EVEN MADE A CAKE TO CHEER UP THE CAR WHEN IT NEEDED BRAKES...
"THE BEST WAS WHEN SHE SPRAYED HERSELF WITH INSECTICIDE 'CAUSE SHE HAD 'ANTS IN HER PANTS'!"
HAH!
HEY, WENDY!... MOM AND DAD WANT TO SEE YOU.
WHAT DO THEY WANT *NOW?*
THEY'RE GOING TO GIVE YOU A NEW VIDEO GAME, BECAUSE YOUR GRADES ARE SO GOOD.
AWESOME!
GAK!
OR MAYBE THEY'RE TAKING THE OLD ONE AWAY 'CAUSE HER GRADES ARE SO BAD...
...I GET EVERYTHING MIXED UP.
CAZENOVE & WILLIAM

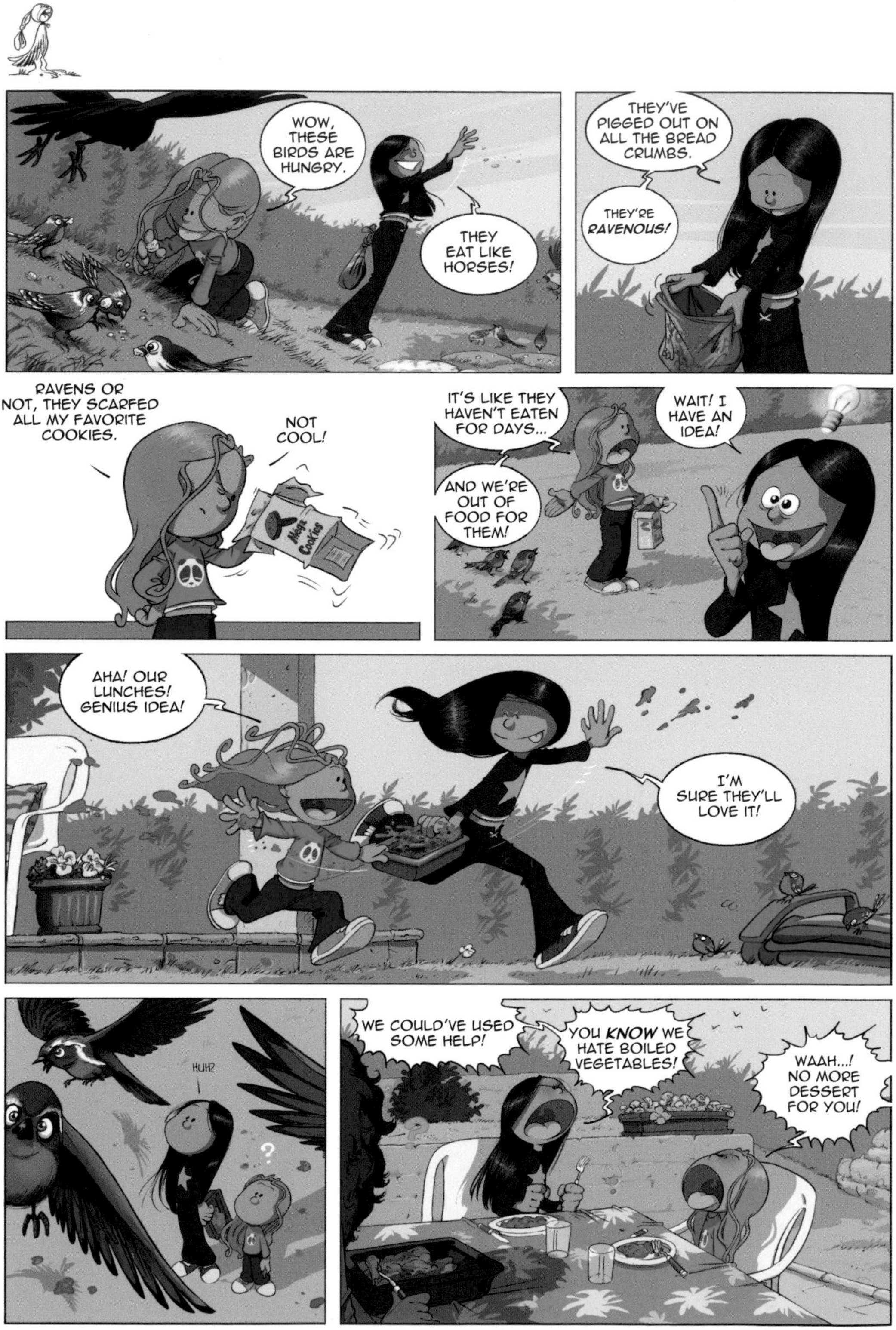
WOW, THESE BIRDS ARE HUNGRY.
THEY EAT LIKE HORSES!
THEY'VE PIGGED OUT ON ALL THE BREAD CRUMBS.
THEY'RE RAVENOUS!
RAVENS OR NOT, THEY SCARFED ALL MY FAVORITE COOKIES.
NOT COOL!
Méga Cookies
IT'S LIKE THEY HAVEN'T EATEN FOR DAYS...
AND WE'RE OUT OF FOOD FOR THEM!
WAIT! I HAVE AN IDEA!
AHA! OUR LUNCHES! GENIUS IDEA!
I'M SURE THEY'LL LOVE IT!
HUH?
?
WE COULD'VE USED SOME HELP!
YOU **KNOW** WE HATE BOILED VEGETABLES!
WAAH...! NO MORE DESSERT FOR YOU!
CAZENOVE & WILLIAM